A FROG'S-
EYE VIEW

A Richard Jackson Book

Also by Rebecca Busselle
BATHING UGLY

A FROG'S-EYE VIEW

REBECCA BUSSELLE

ORCHARD BOOKS • NEW YORK

Orchard Books
A division of Franklin Watts, Inc.
387 Park Avenue South
New York, NY 10016

"Me and Bobby McGee" by Kris Kristofferson
and Fred Foster
© 1969 Temi Combine Inc. All rights controlled by Combine
Music Corp. and administered by EMI Blackwood Music Inc.
All rights reserved. International copyright secured. Used by
permission.

Manufactured in the United States of America
Book design by Mina Greenstein
The text of this book is set in 11 pt. Janson.
10 9 8 7 6 5 4 3 2 1

Library of Congress Cataloging-in-Publication Data
Busselle, Rebecca, A frog's eye view /
by Rebecca Busselle. p. cm.
Summary: Neela's aged aunt helps her to deal with her feelings
of jealousy and self-destructiveness when her idyllic summer
with boy friend Nick is spoiled when he gets a day job and
acquires a female singer for his band.
ISBN 0-531-05907-3.   ISBN 0-531-08507-4 (lib. bdg.)
[1. Aunts—Fiction.] I. Title. PZ7.B9664Fr 1990
[Fic]—dc20 90-30645 CIP AC

for
AUNT PAT
and
in memory of
HAZEL STRAND

A FROG'S-EYE VIEW

ONE

"**N**eela! Open up quickly. Here I come!"

I lunged for the doorknob, and Susannah, my mother, staggered into my bedroom. She was winded, panting as though she'd just hauled a refrigerator up seven flights of stairs. In her arms she balanced three empty cardboard boxes. The cartons slid down to the faded oriental rug. She pinched a check between her thumb and fingers like a lobster claw going after human flesh—a check for selling yet another piece of my bedroom furniture.

"Whew. Give me—" she gasped—"a second to get my breath back."

I looked around at my desk, my bureau, my dressing table, my bed, the little antique table in the bay window. "What's going this time?"

Susannah blotted her forehead with the back of one hand, pressing her other hand to her ribs. The check rose and fell with each breath just below her heart.

"Start packing." She nodded at the bureau. "Begin at the top."

For the past six months I'd stored my clothes in a

mahogany dresser that consisted of seven smooth-sliding drawers with little brass cherubs for knobs. It was known as a highboy in the antique world because it was tall—originally used, Susannah told me, in the dining rooms of elegant eighteenth-century houses to store embroidered linens. In our St. Louis house, the highboy had held my underwear, sweaters, T-shirts, shorts, and jeans.

I stood on tiptoe, raking around at eye level in the top drawer. As I collected a fistful of cuffed-together socks, I pushed the little picture of my boyfriend Nick deep into a back corner of the drawer.

"That dull, dull Mrs. Babcock. I can hardly believe it."

I threw the socks in a cardboard box, then shut the drawer quickly, as though it were empty. *Nick was safe.*

"She's been coming here every couple of months for years," Susannah droned on. "Examining every stick of furniture. Pointing out every worn spot on a rug, turning over every piece of china to check the marks. Boring me to death with her chatter and questions. And she never bought so much as a vase. Never spent a penny."

"Susannah," I began, trying to get her attention. I'd always called my mother Susannah and my father Leonard; when I was a kid I tried not to call them anything in front of my friends, because they had *mommies*, with a few *mummies* thrown in, and of course there were *daddies* and one had a *pops*. Now that I was seventeen, my friends thought it was great I called my parents by their first names—a sign of maturity somehow. To them it implied friendship among equals.

"But at last all my patience has paid off, and I mean

2

paid off!" Susannah crowed. She crinkled up her lips and kissed the check.

"Susannah, please," I tried again, "what am I supposed to do with my clothes?"

Susannah's hands were on her hips, and she wiggled back and forth in small, self-satisfied swings. "But I must admit," she continued, "when she came through, old Bertha Babcock came through in a big way—and showed decent taste, too."

"Susannah. You want me to put my stuff in these boxes. Then what? Are you going to get me some more drawers?" I tried to keep my voice matter-of-fact, so she wouldn't accuse me of whining.

"She's going to buy more in the future, you mark my words. I'll put her on my tea list, that's what I'll do."

Since my mother had become an antiques dealer, selling furniture, prints and drawings, silver, rugs—all of it out of our house—she gave monthly teas for her clients. Before each of these events, she'd press me into service, baking crisp lace cookies. Together we'd shine up the silver tea service. I'd pull a stool up to the pantry counter and listen to her lecture on antiques as we worked the pink-paste silver polish into the scrollwork of a creamer with a soft square of flannel. It was then she most often proclaimed that antiques were treasured possessions, which could best be appreciated in a gracious setting. *Our* gracious setting. That's why, rather than spend hundreds of dollars each month to rent a store, she'd turned our home into her warehouse and showroom.

"Hey, Susannah." Again I thought how easy it would be to say *Mom*, a short word that could be an attention-getting little explosion, while *Susannah* dragged softly on

3

and on in hushed syllables. "Where am I supposed to put my things?"

"Sweetie, do you know what a check this size means?" She didn't want an answer: she charged right ahead. "Mad money of the best kind. A trip, perhaps—Bermuda! That's it, Bermuda this winter, when I'm too ground down by the weather."

Winter. It was barely summer—by calendar standards it wouldn't be summer until the solstice, the twenty-first of June, still two days away. However, heat already saturated St. Louis and wrung it like a steaming towel. The last few days of school had been unbearable—exams taken in a classroom where the sun pounded through tall windows and tortured my neck and shoulders. Then, three days ago, the buzzer ending classes went off for the last time this term. If you judged by school time, the summer—freedom—had just begun.

"OK—" my voice dropped with resignation—"I'll just pack up these boxes and stack them by the door until I get a new dresser."

"Oh no, that won't do." At last I had Susannah's attention. She twisted the scarab ring she always wore for luck, which she claimed was from the tomb of some pharaoh. "It looks tacky to have boxes around. We've got to keep your room the treasure that it is; don't forget, we have some important clients coming this week." Susannah spoke in the plural, as though her business were our joint venture. "Put them in your closet, for now. I've got my eye on a gorgeous French country chest that will be perfect in here."

She leaned down, bending at the knees to keep her skirt from riding up the back of her legs, and pulled open my bottom drawer. "How much space do you need any-

4

way, Neela?" She plucked out a pair of shorts and rubbed them between her fingers, as though they were made of some exotic fabric she was considering using for upholstery material. Then she looked suspiciously at me. "Are all these clothes really yours?"

Susannah and Leonard had started me on a clothing allowance when I was ten. I knew every sweater in my drawer, from the blue cardigan with cables that had been the last thing my grandmother knitted before she died, to the black mohair I'd bought last fall when I started going out with Nick. Compared to my friends I didn't have that many clothes, but I shopped devotedly for what I had and took good care of them all. Sweaters were protected by plastic bags. Shoes were neatly arranged in a row in my closet. And Susannah had taught me to hang hangers on the closet pole with the hook facing the back, so in case of fire they could be removed in one armload.

Susannah knew the clothes were all mine, so she didn't wait for an answer. "Well, pack them up. We'll figure something out. But the important thing is to keep this room tidy for the clients."

As soon as she'd gone downstairs I snatched the photograph of Nick from the top drawer. There he was, not all stiff and fake as he looked in yearbook class pictures, but the way he was with me. Bertie Albrecht, his next door neighbor, had taken the photograph in his living room, and Nick had given it to me right after we started going out. He sat on the couch, arm draped over the back; whenever I looked at that picture I saw a space where I could snuggle next to him. He seemed to be waiting for me. His eyes were soft; the corners of his lips looked ready to smile or form a kiss.

I stroked the satin surface, then hid it again, this time

in a desk drawer under an old sketchbook and a tin box of watercolors.

I flopped on the bed. An earthquake trembled up through the fluted poles and frame of the canopy. As I watched the fringe shake, I thought how often I'd heard about how we have to be careful with antique furniture, and how we never really own anything. "It's all just loaned to us." Those were Susannah's words, and whenever I heard them, I silently added the words "for money." Loaned to us for money.

But I wanted to own something. Before my mother became an antiques dealer, we had furniture that was ours, a little shabby perhaps—compared to some of the tonier families on Arlington Place—but ours. Then Susannah decided that she wanted more money. Leonard's investment business bought the groceries—and good ones—but the extra income would put us right up there. She became the antiques queen.

My childhood bed had been a plain box spring and mattress sitting in a metal frame. Susannah replaced it with a bed shaped like an old-fashioned sleigh. In it I had wonderful dreams of snowstorms and white, blue-eyed dogs. One day when I came home from school, two huge men were easing the bed down the stairs, and it was off, to shape someone else's wintry dreams.

I spent a few nights on a mattress on the floor, then Susannah moved in something that seemed more like a couch than a bed, with a curved wooden back. I remember the word "Empire." It had a horsehair seat from which needlelike fibers would work their way through the upholstery and into my skin if I wiggled around. I kept my sheets and blankets in the closet, made up the couch-bed every night, and fell asleep praying someone would buy it.

I slept in a couple of other beds before I got this one—the four-poster with a canopy. Susannah said there used to be a real reason for canopy beds—dirt falling from the ceilings of castles—but now they're only for decoration. But when I lay under the canopy I felt safe, as though I was crawling into a tent that would keep trouble off me. I had the same feeling when I was little and hid under a sheet-covered old table stored on our third floor.

This year I'd felt that there was more than dirt falling from the castle ceiling; there were huge boulders crashing down from the sky. Everything was changing.

Next year I'd be a senior in the school I'd gone to since first grade. After that I was expected to march on to college. Already people were asking what field I was planning to major in, when I didn't know *where* I wanted to go, or really even *if* I wanted to go. This year had been a terror of aptitude tests and achievement tests, a nightmare of parents and advisors and guidance counselors warning me about how much junior-year grades count with admissions committees. I believed them. But how did I know if all the studying and cramming and extra projects were worth it—for something that was going to happen year after next?

Even in our house, things were changing. A relative had moved into our third floor. Her name was Amelia —my real name—and Leonard and Susannah thought because we were both Amelias that meant it was OK for her to take over the only part of the house I felt was mine.

I hated the name Amelia. Leonard's family had had one in every generation since umpteen-hundred. I hated it so much that when I was six I began to call myself Neela. I can remember lying in that plain, snug little metal-frame bed saying "Neela" over and over—now and then tossing in an "Amelia" to test it against.

Neela was my own name. No one else had it. I didn't know this Amelia, but she was Leonard's aunt. All he'd ever said about her was that she'd lived in New York all her life, her husband had recently died, and she was depressed. Since she'd moved in two weeks ago, the door to the third floor was tightly closed. She didn't come out at night, and since I'd been at school all day and studying like crazy on the weekend, I hadn't seen her.

I opened another drawer of the highboy—one of the last times I would feel the scrunched little face of the cherub with my thumb and the wings that grew from his tiny shoulders between my fingers. I took out my T-shirts. Two of them were from concerts Nick and I'd gone to together. I always kept these folded so I could see "The Boss"—Bruce Springsteen—and my favorite, James Taylor, as soon as I opened the drawer. Nick had given me a Grateful Dead T-shirt, which I kept under my other ones and hadn't had the nerve to wear yet. I wasn't sure Susannah knew who the Grateful Dead were, but I was afraid that if she saw the skull and roses she'd freak out.

But the hardest thing for me right now was the fear that Nick was changing. I didn't know why I felt that way, but I did. I'd called him yesterday because I hadn't heard from him since the end of school. His mother, Mrs. Cunningham, said he was out, but she'd leave him a message. She was reliable. I could feel my fear in the silence of the telephone.

I packed my jeans and corduroy pants in a different carton, the one that could go in the back of my closet or bottom of my chest or whatever came next, because it was summer and I wouldn't need those clothes for three months.

Last summer Leonard had arranged a volunteer job for me at a big downtown hospital, because he was chairman of the fund-raising committee. "It might give you something substantial to write your college application essay on," he'd said. So every morning I had put on a pink and white striped smock and got into my little orange Volkswagen Bug.

It had been Susannah's car, but she'd given it to me for my sixteenth birthday. I was the envy of my friends. Susannah said she hated to part with it because it was an antique, but now that she was in business she needed a station wagon like Leonard's to cart around all the stuff she bought. I knew that one reason I got the car was that she hated to drive me anywhere.

And so I drove myself to the hospital, usually taking the slow way through Forest Park, then getting on the old highway that took me past huge grain-storage silos and bridged over a railroad yard. When I smelled the sweet stench of a meat-processing house, I was there. Inside the high-rise hospital, I sold candy in the gift shop with two women Susannah's age and never saw a patient. It wouldn't fly as an essay on "my most significant experience."

But this summer would be something to write about. This would be my summer with Nick. Maybe this *chang-*

ing idea was all in my head. There could be dozens of reasons why he hadn't called.

Leonard's station wagon turned off the avenue and advanced between the open iron gates that stood sentry at both ends of our street, Arlington Place. This section of the city was an enclave of "private blocks." The end that ran into the avenue was always closed to traffic. The sidewalk gates were locked with chains and padlocks, and only the residents had keys. Sharp ornamental curlicues topped those gates, but some others were less subtle— iron spikes, a straight row of vertical spears. Leonard said the gates were there to protect us. Certainly the neighborhood's message was clear: If you don't have business on the block, you're not welcome.

I sat on the front steps, the heat from the cement radiating up my shorts and bare feet. My fingernails scratched away at a tormenting spider bite on my knee. I'd left the front door open, so I could hear the phone when it rang; only the screen door guarded the house.

My father drove down the block slowly, his wheels easing over each yellow safety bump like Petunia, our neighbors' dachshund, waddling over the curb, belly low to the ground. The bumps stretched the width of the street. They'd been put in when I was a kid because a speeding florist truck, delivering flowers for Shelby Moran's debutante party, had gone pedal-to-the-metal and knocked one of my friends off her bike. Now everyone crept along, except for a few die-hards who found the fifty feet between bumps a sprint-derby challenge. I was especially cautious in my ancient VW Bug, because the chassis was so battered and the parts so hard to replace.

Leonard parked in front of the house. I waved, but he was busy gathering his briefcase and suit jacket.

"Scorcher, huh?" he muttered, as he trudged up the front walk. He always looked bushed when he came home from work, his gray hair straggling over his forehead, bow tie pulled apart, and shirt collar unbuttoned. Even his horn-rimmed glasses looked ready to fall off. He walked toward me up the steps. Just short of my toes, he leaned over and scratched the top of my head, his fingers sifting absently through my hair to my scalp. It was the way he'd greeted me every day, always, and I loved the brittle sound it made—as though my head had turned to sand. Then he turned aside and skirted around me.

"Hey there Leonard," I said to his retreating back.

"Hi Neela," he replied. It took him such a long time to say this—as though he had to think up something original—that by the time it came out he was on the granite stoop of our house.

I knew he'd revive as soon as he went inside. The pattern was always the same: He'd holler for Susannah. From somewhere, perhaps the kitchen, my mother summoned him. And then there was silence. I knew he'd found her, and he'd kiss her forehead and the tip of her nose.

They must have been in the kitchen, because the dogs got all excited. Half of the backyard was a kennel which Leonard had built for his three strong and wiry hunters. Now that the dogs knew he was home, they began to bark in high, excited yelps, hurling themselves against the chain-link kennel walls. Their yaps whined up and down like heavy metal, and their body-flinging crashes boomed like out-of-control drums.

11

I knew what was happening next. Leonard would be taking the dented tin dog pans from the counter, lined with scraps from last night's supper, as well as morning bacon grease. He'd mix in dog food. Then I knew he was on his way to the kennel, because the slamming and yelping settled into throaty barking, and then quiet.

Through all this I listened, with no luck, for the ring of the phone.

In the pantry, I watched Leonard make martinis. He put ice cubes in a glass pitcher and poured gin from a quart bottle. He bent over the pitcher to check the level against an invisible mark. With great concentration, he added a few drops of vermouth. He stirred this concoction with a glass rod. "Always stir gently," he told me. "Gin bruises easily." Once, when I was younger, I sneaked downstairs at night and poured some gin violently from glass to glass, waiting for it to bruise. Instead of turning blue and purple, it stayed clear.

Leonard put an olive in each of two stemmed glasses, and, with impressive care, poured the drinks. Then he put everything—the pitcher, the glasses, the bowl of olives, the little napkins, my glass of orange juice—on a lacquered tray, and gave it to me to carry while he let in the dogs.

In the living room I settled into my favorite chair, which had a lion's head carved at the end of each armrest, and lion's paws with gigantic toenails at the bottom of the stumpy legs. The dogs bounded into the kitchen.

"Make them behave, Leonard," Susannah called.

Our downstairs had become the main showroom of Susannah's antique business. The drama began as you entered the house. The only items in the hall—a large room—were a choice Persian rug and a massive oak table that held a single Chinese lamp and, on a round, silver plate, Susannah's business cards. When she'd started her enterprise, I'd suggested some names: *Susannah's Attic*, or something catchy like *Silver 'n' Old*. She rejected these ideas. Her thick cream-colored cards said *Susannah Stokes: Dealer in Antiquity* in raised, lavender script. I thought it made her sound early Greek, but she liked it.

But if the hall was spare, the other rooms more than made up for it. The living room, where we had cocktails, was jammed with all varieties of chairs, couches, and occasional tables loaded with Tiffany lamps, inlaid wood cigarette boxes, silver candlesticks—all stuff for sale. The dining room actually had two tables end to end and three sideboards. In the room Susannah still called "the library," she had removed every book from the shelves and filled them with teapots and china plates displayed on wire stands. Above them, prints of fox hunts competed for wall space with oil portraits of the stern-faced ancestors of strangers.

There were only two rooms off limits to the antique customers: the kitchen, where Leonard kept his scrap-filled dog pans, and Leonard's den, which was as crammed as the rest of the house, with duck decoys and hunting prints.

The dogs burst through the house and into the living room, their tails wagging like whips, snuffling the rugs, knocking into table legs. They were tough, passionate work dogs. The two field dogs loved roaming the countryside with Leonard, sniffing for the scent of quail or doves, and when they found them, waiting with great discipline, tails in the air, pointing, until Leonard gave them the signal to flush out the birds. The retriever loved sitting for hours in freezing duck blinds, then swimming through icy water to pick up dead birds.

They all loved Leonard. Each had a pedigree name —Thunder of Hillsdale or something equally monumental—and Leonard had short names for them— like King. But I called the dogs Liver, Bacon, and Onions. Liver was exactly that color, purple-red. Bacon had a wrinkled forehead that made him look as though he'd been fried. Onions smelled.

Bacon ran into the bathroom—the powder room, Susannah had renamed it—and slurped from the toilet, dribbling on the hall rug as he ran out. Liver tried to sniff my feet, but I quickly tucked them under me.

"Feet off the furniture," Susannah reminded me. Then she appealed to Leonard. "Make then *behave*, darling." She sipped her drink.

"All right," he shouted in command tone. "I want all you dogs to *sit*." And sit they did, tongues dripping from their mouths, panting, looking up at their master with expectation. "Now lie down," he thundered. They melted around his ankles, and for a few minutes there was peace in the house.

I let my feet slide down the chair legs, curling my soles over the lion's paws and trying to fit my toes into the crevices between their nails. Leonard talked about accounts. I pulled at the frayed edge of my cut-offs. Leonard talked about portfolios and gross income. I scratched at the spider bite on my knee. Now that I was out of school, no one asked if I'd done my biology homework, or whether I was still reading *Othello* for

English. "Dull, dull, Bertha Babcock," I heard Susannah say. I willed the phone to ring: *Make Nick call me, make Nick call me.*

"Has Aunt Amelia been out today?" Leonard asked Susannah.

"Amelia? Not that I know of. Neela? Has she?"

I was startled to hear my name. "I don't think so. I really haven't been paying much attention. But I've been around all day." Around the phone all day. And who cared if Aunt Amelia had been out or not?

"I'm worried about her," Leonard said.

"Is there a tad left?" Susannah asked, nodding at the glass martini pitcher.

Leonard put new olives in each glass and poured, holding back ice with one finger. "A tad" meant another big drink for both of them.

Once, last year, I took the tray back to the kitchen when they'd finished and drained the leftovers in the pitcher. The ice had melted and diluted the gin, but even so it puckered my mouth and burned right down my throat to my stomach. It was powerful stuff.

"There's nothing to worry about, darling." Susannah's voice was beginning to sound thick, as though she had a sponge in her throat. "Amelia wants privacy. She said so when we made this arrangement."

"I know, but this is isolation, not just privacy." He smacked his palm on the table next to him, making his drink slosh over onto the cocktail napkin. I thought how strange it was that while they both drank the same drink, Susannah became heavier and slower, while Leonard became pushy.

"There's nothing to be done about her, nothing at

all." Susannah's tone was petulant. "Amelia pays rent, and I'm not going to interfere in her life."

"There's a difference between not interfering and being irresponsible."

"Oh?" The word trailed out like a long, dull knife, slicing through Susannah's heavy voice. "You think I'm irresponsible?"

I looked out the window. Across the street the Steiner boys were coming out of their house with skateboards. I'd been a roller skater at their age, and I could remember the feeling of every sidewalk square on both sides of the block; the new ones were smooth as oil, but the gritty, pocked old ones sent electric jolts up your calves.

"You're not irresponsible." Leonard's voice was growly. "I never said *you* were irresponsible."

Liver, Onions, and Bacon got up from Leonard's feet and wandered out into the hall. I snapped my fingers to call them over for a pat, but they ignored me.

"She's your aunt," Susannah said. "Go up and talk to her if you're so worried."

"I might just do that."

The kids skateboarded past our house doing tricks. From the hall there was pandemonium as the dogs barked at them, heaving their bodies against the screen door, which had long ago been reinforced with heavy wire mesh.

"All right!" Leonard was on his feet yelling. "Knock it off! You get right back in here!" And the dogs obeyed, making tight circles and sinking again at my father's feet.

"Neela!" He was still shouting, as though I was one of the dogs. That voice made me wish I could lie quietly on the rug out of his attention. "Neela! Go upstairs and tell Aunt Amelia to come down for a cocktail."

16

I didn't want to have anything to do with Aunt Amelia. For weeks before she moved in, workmen had tramped up and down to the third floor, dirtying the tarps that Susannah had made them spread over the stairs and halls. They built new partitions and reworked plumbing and wiring. They painted and refinished the floors. Susannah insisted on keeping me up to date on the renovations. I asked no questions; I didn't want details. Susannah had rented—for money, of course—my beloved third floor.

It had never been an attic. All the houses on Arlington Place were chunky and large. Some were made of a dull, yellow brick, like ours, while others were rust-colored brick, and a few had a smooth, stucco-gray finish. Some had columns that rose two stories, like ours, and some had porches. But they all had third floors. Leonard had grown up in this house and bought it from "the estate" when my grandparents died. And my grandfather had grown up in it too, and so had his sister, Aunt Amelia.

When my grandfather lived here everyone on Arlington Place was wealthy. Leonard said they used to have a "couple" who lived on the third floor and did the cooking, the cleaning, and the yard work. By now "couples" and servants were long gone. Though some families had made their third floors into playrooms, and one rented theirs to a college student, most, like us, used them for storage. Before Susannah decided to sell everything, we had kept my grandparents' old furniture up there.

Susannah had saved all the dresses she'd ever liked; they filled two big closets. Each year I measured how much I'd grown by how her clothes fit. Susannah's minidresses from the sixties were ball gowns on me when I was five; but by the time I was twelve I was taller than she was, and her fanciest dresses, the long ones, floated an inch above the ground. I'd tramped around in her old shoes when my heel only came halfway up the arch: now they were all too small.

The dusty, rose-colored rooms crammed with my grandparents' furniture, the closets, the boxes of old books, the bathroom with the sink stained turquoise where water had dripped from the copper fixtures—all this I'd considered mine. Then Susannah took out the furniture and began selling it. But the rooms were still mine. Then she told me she was renovating the third floor and Aunt Amelia was moving in. The closets were emptied. The bathroom ripped out.

I kept my eyes on the red, shiny spider bite on my knee. I had to answer Leonard. If I could keep my voice neutral, keep out the complaining tone—as I had earlier with Susannah—I might have a chance. I knew how whining annoyed them both. Perhaps the pure truth would allow them room for mercy. "I'm sorry, but I just can't go up there," I said apologetically.

"Excuse me, young lady? Just what did you say? You *can't*? You mean you *won't*." Leonard took off his glasses and laid them on the table.

Suddenly Susannah jumped sides. "That's right, young lady. There's a lonely old woman upstairs—how can you refuse to invite her down?"

Young lady? We were Susannah and Leonard and Neela; we were partners in business; we were equals. Leonard always said he didn't believe in talking down to children. He'd taught me to make a martini when I was eight; he took me hunting when I was twelve; he let me drive the car around the block when I was thirteen. Young lady?

I knew I'd have to go up there. But I could stall for time.

"What am I supposed to say?" I tried to sound innocent, not dumb. Nothing irritated them more than stupidity.

Leonard put his glasses back on. "Say, my dear, that we want her to come down for a cocktail." His words were even.

"But aren't you finished with cocktails? Isn't it almost dinner time?"

"We can always adjust our schedule, Neela." Susannah began looking through an issue of *Art and Antiques*.

I studied the small lumps of ice remaining in the glass pitcher and had a suspicion I knew what she meant by adjusting her schedule.

I started up the staircase. A red carpet led to the second floor, "to make the customer feel like royalty," Susannah said. At the top, the landing had become a gallery of prints—sailboats and yachts—and I stopped to examine a couple. I glanced wistfully at the closed door to my room.

The stairway to the third floor was narrow and bare. I walked up slowly, and when I reached the door at the top, realized I'd come so quietly the old lady might be frightened to hear a knock. So I crept down and tramped up again, bumping into the wall and sounding as heavy as my bare feet would allow. I knocked with my knuckles.

A very tall, thin woman opened the door immediately. I barely glanced at her. What I cared about was looking beyond her into my dusty, rosy hideaway. Which was no more.

"Yes?" she said.

Beyond her I could see a stark white wall and a floor so clean and varnished it seemed to be a reflection of itself.

"I'm Neela."

The only pieces of furniture appeared to be a black leather couch with chrome legs, a glass table, and in a corner by the window, a wooden rocking chair.

"Oh?"

"Neela. You know, the same as you—Amelia."

"Really." She moved a step closer to me, blocking the doorway as though she knew I was trying to look in. Now we were face to face, and I found myself transfixed by her pale, wrinkled cheeks, and the heavy makeup she had caked around her eyes. "And what may I do for you, Amelia?"

"Neela." A bead of sweat escaped from my temple and dripped in front of my ear. I could feel the coolness of the air-conditioned room behind her. "My parents want you to come down for a cocktail."

"I see." She considered this for a moment, rubbing her finger over puckered lips. "Well, thank your parents for their kind invitation, but I think I'll decline. I'm not much of a drinker."

That was it, I had done my duty, I could go. I started to turn.

"Are you?" she asked.

"Am I? Am I what?"

"Much of a drinker."

I remembered the martini pitcher, the clear liquid

which looked harmless as water, with the biting taste and fiery feeling. "No," I said, and for some reason I smiled. "That's not exactly how I'd describe myself."

I was halfway down the stairs when she called, "And tell your parents I'm just fine."

And then I ran all the way down both flights of stairs, because the dogs were barking, and through their racket, I thought I heard the doorbell ring.

TWO

It wasn't mere barking, it was open jaws and growls and snarls and ear-splitting hacks. The dogs hurled themselves at the screen door, shaking the frame, straining the wire mesh. I prayed the hinges would hold. Those beasts meant business. Leonard came into the hall from the living room, and blocked the door with his body and outstretched arm.

"Now!" he shouted. "All of you sit, and I mean it!" The way his voice roared out into the street, I expected to see all the neighbors down on their haunches.

When the dogs were sitting, pink tongues slobbering and pulsing with obedience, Leonard looked away from them and up at me. "It's for you," he said, as though a package had been delivered. He walked into the living room, Bacon, Liver, and Onions at his heels.

I turned the screen door handle and went outside. My heart beat an odd, irregular rhythm; my breath came in little gulps.

Nick wasn't standing directly in front of the screen; he had bolted to the side of the stoop for protection and gripped the iron railing, ready to vault and flee. Beyond him, Arlington Place was quiet now, though after all that noise the stillness seemed to resonate, like muscles that twitch after death.

"Hi," I said into the silence.

Nick just looked at me without moving.

I didn't know what to do next. After waiting and waiting these past days, I felt shy and uncomfortable. But oh, how good it was to see him.

"Wow," he said at last, "those hounds are quite a way to say have-a-good-day. Talk about taking your life in your hands."

"How did you get here?" I asked.

Clearly, I'd just uttered one of my silly, space-filling questions. Tight Lycra bicycle shorts hugged his thighs. They were his one concession to trendy sports attire, and he'd said he only wore them because they made biking more comfortable. His shirt was an old, faded, striped rugby shirt that had seen lots of sun. He held a shiny white helmet by its chin strap. It was clear how he got here.

Nick nodded at the racing bike propped against a sycamore tree. "Thirty-seven minutes from my house to yours." He pushed the button that reset his triathlon watch from stop-time back to regular time.

"It's too hot for a bike today." Again, my words sounded lame, but I couldn't let him know the pleasure I felt that he'd ride at full speed, thirty-seven minutes through this heat, to see me. "Do you want to come in and have something to drink?"

"It's OK, never mind. I wouldn't face those mutts again for a million bucks. Anyway, I've got water." He nodded again toward the bike, and I saw a white water bottle clipped to the frame. "Let's sit someplace."

We didn't have a porch with wicker chairs like the Donovans up the street, and though we had a front lawn, the grass was dotted with brown pee spots. Nick folded down onto the cement steps; then I sat, close to him, our hips lightly touching. I loved the glow I felt whenever my body rubbed against his.

He pushed himself up on his hands and shifted over a few inches. "Like you said, it's a hot day."

But I had to touch him—I always had to touch him. He let me fluff the damp curls that were flattened on his forehead, shaking his head to help me. His hair was dark enough to be called black, although when the light caught it, I could see glints of brown and red, and every so often blue. His curls licked the edges of his ears and the back of his neck, and sometimes when we were alone, with one finger I would trace the precise line where hair and skin meet.

"So, what's going on?" he asked.

Before I could answer, I heard a fumble at the screen door latch, and Leonard stepped out. "Neela," he began.

"Hello, Mr. Stokes," Nick said, getting to his feet and turning around.

"Nick." Leonard nodded in bare acknowledgment. And back to me. "Neela, where's Amelia? Isn't she coming down?"

"Whoops, I forgot to tell you. She said she's fine and you shouldn't worry about her and thanks for your invitation, but she's going to hold on it." I didn't mention that she wasn't much of a drinker.

"In that case dinner will be in twenty minutes." He

didn't look at Nick. He didn't ask if he'd already eaten, or if he'd like to join us. "Twenty minutes," he repeated.

"So what's going on?" Nick asked again, when Leonard had shut the door. He always acted as though my father hadn't ignored him. Every time I tried to apologize for Leonard, Nick just shrugged and said it was no big deal. He didn't seem to take it personally. He seemed more offended by the way the dogs carried on than by Leonard's curt and crusty mode. "What've you been up to?"

"Well, it hasn't been exactly a ball around here." I scratched at my spider bite again, but kept my voice light. "First Susannah had me put everything I own into cardboard boxes and pack it all away so she could sell the furniture in my room."

"That sounds like a drag."

"Then I had to deal with this great-aunt who's moved in upstairs."

"So you've finally met her? What's she like?"

"Weird. Tons of makeup and arty clothes. No one you'd want to spend a lot of time with."

I kept my eyes on the bite. The whole area around it had the thin, parched look of waxed paper. "And worst of all—" I traced an imaginary tear rolling down my cheek—"you didn't call me back yesterday."

There was no reaction from Nick.

"All of which means that so far it's not my idea of a great summer vacation."

"Poor Neela," he said at last, staring at the bite on my knee. "Someone better take care of you." He swung my leg over his and smoothed the inflamed skin around the bite with his thumbs, as though he was about to perform some sort of surgery. Under my calf, I could feel every hair on his thigh, every pore, with the intensity of stepping barefoot into warm grass after a long winter. He took a pen from his shirt pocket and slowly drew a line on my knee around the bite. A tickle burned through the itching.

I began to laugh.

"Don't move," he said, and tightened his grip on my leg. "There," he said when he'd finished. He hoisted my leg back; I examined my knee. He'd drawn a circle around the white pustule of the bite and written in capital letters: DON'T SCRATCH.

"Neela," he said, his voice gently dropping down a tone, "I didn't call back because I was busy. It's not about you. I've just got a lot of things going this summer, you know."

"Of course I know. I've got a lot planned, too." But I didn't. I'd saved the summer for Nick.

"For openers, I've got to find a job, at least part-time. There's not going to be much fun if there isn't any cash."

Susannah had offered me a part-time job, baby-sitting the house while she was at auctions or out making deals. She wanted someone there to answer the phone because she said customers liked the personal touch, not answering machines. And sometimes furniture was delivered or picked up, which meant the delivery men had to pass the kennel on their way to the back door. No one would dare walk near those dogs without being reassured that they were really locked up.

"I'm thinking of doing something part-time myself," I said.

"I can always get a job packing groceries or stocking

shelves at the supermarket, but that's not what I'm looking for." Nick rolled the pen between his palms, as I'd seen him do so often in school when he was working over a calculus problem, or waiting for inspiration on an English test. "I'd like something that pays a little better, that's for sure. But the most important thing is to have my head filled. I can't stand the idea of being bored this summer."

Bored? How could that word even come to him when summer meant there would be time for us to be together? Time to take long drives to the river, to have picnics, to go to movies and hang out at his house and find secret places to be alone. How could he even imagine being bored?

Nick knew what I was thinking, I was sure he did. His eyes were sometimes the soft blue of twilight and other times an amazing, sharp blue; when he looked at me the way he did now, they seemed to get brighter, like light bulbs in a power surge.

"Nick," I finally said, "there's no way you're going to be bored this summer."

"Right. Even if I find a dull job, that'll give me head space to write some new songs. And I've talked to a couple of guys who live in my neighborhood—a drummer and a keyboard player—who want to get together and jam in the evenings." Then he either paused, or his words came at a different pace. "And Bertie wants to try vocals with me, so I'm going to let her."

Bertie. The one who took the picture of Nick with soft eyes. I fiddled with my turquoise ring, twirling the stone around my finger. My hand wandered to my knee, but I saw Nick's antiscratching warning just in time. I would stay in neutral; I wouldn't let my heart flop around.

Nick was a good student at school; we both were. He was strong in science and math—next year he'd be taking advanced placement courses in physics and calculus—while I struggled, staying up late with homework and going to teachers for extra help, to get decent grades in Algebra II and biology. But I could write a history paper, or analyze a poem with an ease that made him envious, and I'd been elected next year's editor of *The Guardian*, the weekly school newspaper.

Nick played first string on the varsity soccer and basketball teams and trained on his bike as an independent sport in spring. I played wing in field hockey (we went to the state finals last fall), took volleyball in winter, and recently began running cross-country, though my time wasn't all that good.

Where we split apart was theatrical talent. If I even thought about getting up on a stage, it would be to play a tree in a hurricane, my limbs would be shaking so. But Nick could act. And he could sing. He'd had the lead in our school's winter musical when he was just a sophomore. My voice sounded like a frog having a bad day.

A couple of years ago Nick had moved up from air guitar to the real thing, and though he still wasn't Eric Clapton, he knew the basic chords and practiced his runs and riffs. Also, his singing more than compensated for what he hadn't yet mastered on guitar. His voice had James Taylor's ability to make each note distinct and emphatic, yet effortless.

All through the school year he'd had time for music, and time for me, too.

"Bertie?" I asked. "I didn't know she was a singer."

"I know, it seems weird to me too." He played with his watch, pushing the buttons and setting off little beeps. "I've lived next door to her all my life, and it wasn't until last night that I found out how good she is."

I couldn't say, "Last night?" in the same rhetorical way I'd said, "Bertie?" It was too obvious. And too ludicrous, if I thought about it in any logical way. Last night—while I waited for Nick to call—and Bertie!

"She came over to see if I could give her a hand changing the headlight in her car."

"And that's how you found out she's a singer?"

"We put some tunes into the car stereo while we were working, and she began to sing along. Her voice is pretty good, but what's amazing is that she can harmonize to anything." Nick kept on fiddling with the watch, making the date and time slide past, and the alarm go off.

"Did you get the car fixed?"

"I don't know how she does it. It takes all my concentration to stay on key, and there she is wandering around the melody and sounding great."

"What was it, just the headlight, or some electrical problem, or what?"

"Yeah."

"Yeah what?"

"The headlight." Nick stood up, and shook out his leg, his ankle loose and floppy. A jogger ran down the sidewalk, panting like the melody of a lead singer, while the dull traffic noise from the distant boulevard provided backup.

"Are you going home now?" I asked. I tried to keep dismay from my voice as I watched him strap on his helmet.

"I'm outta here, Neela. You've got to have dinner,

and I want to get home before dark. Thirty-six minutes, this time."

I didn't want to say it, because I was afraid I knew what the answer would be. But I couldn't help myself, I had to ask. "Do you want me to pick you up later? We could go for a drive or something."

"Not tonight. I was up late last night, and I need some sleep. I've got to start looking for a job first thing in the morning." He took his bike from the sycamore tree and popped it off the curb onto the street. I stayed right next to him. He wiggled his left sneaker into the toe clips. "I'll call you sometime tomorrow." He kissed the tips of two fingers, then touched them to my forehead, as though he were blessing me.

"So you'll be at home tonight?" I heard how thin my voice was.

When Nick smiled, his eyes wrinkled at the corners; when he was annoyed, he squinted slightly, and they wrinkled in the same place. "That's what I said."

"Nick, don't be mad."

He looked at me a long moment, then let out his breath. "How can anyone be mad at you? We'll talk tomorrow."

He shoved off with his right foot, and I saw his thighs tighten beneath his Lycra shorts as his left leg pushed hard into the bike pedal—right, left, up, down, the muscles flexing and stretching in his calves, and his old striped shirt billowing at his sides as he pedaled up the block. He straightened one leg to take weight off his seat as he went over the yellow safety bump. Then he picked up speed and turned out through the gates.

• • •

Penelope Radford lived three houses down the block. Both of us had lived on Arlington Place all our lives. The rivalries and torments of competing for playmates when we were little were long behind us. We now considered ourselves too grown up to have "best" friends, but she was certainly my closest friend.

Her parents were always worried about safety and kept their front door locked at all times, even in the middle of summer. Leonard had advised them to get guard dogs—a suggestion they'd declined. Mrs. Radford claimed to be allergic to animals, but I wondered how much they'd been influenced by the barking and shouting up the street. I'd been in and out of their house so often in the past years that when I rang twice—my signature—they'd let me in without putting me through a big greeting ceremony.

I always walked into Penelope's room without knocking. Being together was never an interruption: we were that kind of friends.

"Don't tell me you've been cleaning." The surfaces of her bureau and desk were clear, for a change, while the thick nap of her mossy-green carpet still showed vacuum-cleaner tracks. I clapped my hand to my forehead and reeled around a couple of times before I fainted into her easy chair.

"I had to," she sighed. "Now that school's over, I haven't got the *no time* excuse. Mom said it had to be clean because they might use it as a guest room while I'm gone."

I loved Penelope's room. It was as different from mine as she and I were from each other. First of all, everything was hers—nothing was ever sold. She had snapshots tacked all over the wall above her desk, while I wouldn't dream of displaying my picture of Nick to the world. And Mrs. Radford didn't care if she left soda cans on her bedside table, or didn't hang her dresses up, or let clothes drip out of dresser drawers. When Penelope had one of her occasional neatness spurts, her mom would reward her with something new—like the green rug. Penelope had begged for it; she desperately wanted her floor to look like a pasture.

She always said she was born on a horse, and there was a picture in a silver frame on her dressing table to prove it: a tiny little girl, outfitted in perfect miniature riding attire, was perched, grinning, on a pony. That was Penelope. Years ago she'd stretched a wire across one wall to hold all the rosette-crowned blue ribbons she'd won in horse shows. Shiny trophies gleamed from her bookcase—testaments to what an accomplished rider she was. On the shelf below the trophies was a jumble of horse books that traced her passion, from *Misty of Chincoteague* though *Beginning Dressage*.

I used to watch with envy as she dressed on Saturday mornings to go to the stables, amazed by her transformation from a kid in rumpled jeans to an equestrienne in perfectly fitting jodhpurs. She'd pick up her black velveteen hunt cap while she flicked her crop at me, and she'd be off to the Country Club stables, where she'd sail over jumps.

"So, exactly what time tomorrow do you depart for the wilds of Vermont?" I asked. Penelope was going to be a junior counselor for a month at her riding camp.

"The plane leaves at ten a.m."

"You haven't started packing?"

"There's hardly anything to do. I'm pretty much ready, see?" She opened her closet door, and there on the floor, mixed in with riding boots and Reeboks, was a heap of washed but unfolded clothes. "All I have to do is scoop these into a duffel, and I'm outta here." She jumped onto her bed, landing with her legs crossed Indian-style, her ponytail bouncing behind her.

I slid from the chair to the floor and began doing sit-ups.

"Isn't it a wee bit hot for a workout?" Penelope inquired.

"Your air conditioner's on. And I think I need to tighten up these stomach muscles." My voice was strained with effort. "I'm looking flabby."

"Reality check. You look great. You've got a great body."

"I don't know. I feel fat." I let my breath out in a *whoosh* each time I struggled up. "I may not look it yet, but—"*whoosh*—"that's how I feel."

"What's going on with you? And what are you doing over here at nine o'clock, anyway? I thought you'd be out with Nick."

"He was over earlier." I stopped the sit-ups and lay on the rug, hands still locked behind my neck. "He had to get home because he's going to start looking for a job tomorrow." I couldn't let his phrase, *I was up late last night*, come into my mind. And if it crept in there, I couldn't let it out of my mouth.

"Well, I'm glad you're not going out with him every night. You guys see plenty of each other."

That was a good example of how different Penelope and I are. The contrast between us is deep, and it goes way back. I'd chosen my own name—Neela—because it was short and sounded more normal than Amelia. Penelope, on the other hand, went nuts if someone tried to cut her name down to something more manageable—like *Penny*. And Penelope thought guys were great things to have around, but she didn't want her whole life tied up in one. I'd felt the same way when a boyfriend was only an abstract idea, but now that Nick was in my life, I wanted him with me. And though I couldn't admit it to anyone, I wanted him with me all the time.

"Yeah," I heard myself say, "I could use a couple of nights off." And I realized I could barely concentrate on my own words, because now I was thinking about Nick, and what he was doing by himself tonight, and if he were really home.

"Let's go downstairs and find something to eat," Penelope said.

"Hang on. In a few minutes. I want to ask you something first."

"Shoot."

I tried not to hesitate, because I knew that would give away my nervousness. "What do you think of Bertie?"

"Alberta Albrecht?" She shrugged. "I don't know. She seems like an OK kid. But I've never really hung out with her. Have you?"

"Not really."

"I guess I've always thought of her as a granola bar. The folk music and tofu crowd."

I felt total relief. Of course, that's what she was. Somehow, even though she was in our class at school, she seemed so shadowy that in the last couple of hours I had barely been able to reconstruct what she looked like. And now it all came back—the long, unstyled hair, the Birkenstock sandals with thick leather straps, the dress she sometimes wore with a little apron that made her look as though she'd just stepped out of *The Sound of Music.*

"Are you planning to hang out with her?" Penelope asked.

"Bertie? No. But she lives next door to Nick."

"So? What's that got to do with anything?"

"Nick said she's going to do some singing with a group he's getting together. I guess that means *he'll* be hanging out with her."

"And so you wondered—ever so casually—what she's like."

"Yeah, kind of." I looked at Penelope a little suspiciously. That sarcastic tone of hers usually meant more was coming.

"Oh my goodness—I don't believe it. You're jealous, Neela Stokes. That's what's been . . ."

"Whoa! No way. Jealous of Bertie Albrecht?"

"That's what it sounds like to me. Come on, Neela . . ."

"Stop." I wasn't going to let her finish. "End of conversation. Forget it, Penelope." She enjoyed pinning me to the wall, and it sometimes caused trouble between us. This time she was wrong. *I wasn't jealous; there was nothing to be jealous about; and even if there had been, Bertie Albrecht wouldn't be at the center of it.*

She threw her hands up in surrender. "Okay, sheriff, you've got the gun." Then she fixed me with that intense look of hers that could quiet rampaging horses. "I was just trying to help, you know."

"I know. But things are really OK." Suddenly I wanted to weep, to tell her things weren't OK, I didn't understand what was going on with me, I didn't know why I felt panicked by the thought of being without Nick for even one day. The summer—which I'd so looked forward to—now spun ahead of me, thick and choking as exhaust from a diesel truck.

"All right, I'll believe you if you want me to. But I still think you seem a little shaky."

Suddenly the fact that she couldn't let it go—instead of making me angry or resentful—caused a lump in my throat. She was my true friend. She knew me better than anyone—even Nick. A tear leaked from the corner of my eye, and as I mashed it against the bridge of my nose, I unexpectedly giggled. "Oh Penelope, don't they have another job for me at that camp of yours? I want to go with you. Who cares that I can't ride?"

"Yeah, who cares that you're scared to death of horses?" Penelope hooted.

I stood with knees bent out, my cocked wrists in front of my chest, and posted up and down. "See? I'm as good as you are. Nothing to it, piece of cake."

"Ride that trusty steed! Go girl, go!" She leaped up and began posting next to me, and we moved up and down like two pistons in a motor until we were both laughing so hard that we had to fall. She rolled on her back on the pasture-rug, squirming and neighing with pleasure, and in a second I was doing it too, imagining the dirt and grass scratching my long, horsy spine. That's what it always had been like to be with Penelope: she took me into her fantasy. Even though I'd hated the only two times I'd been on a horse, from the time I was six I could whinny with the best of them and prance with a good, high step.

We lay on the rug, gasping, and she turned her head to look at me. "So, how's it really going between you and Nick?" She wasn't a horse any more, she was my friend.

"I'm not sure. I feel like he's backing off from me." *A few hours ago his hip pressed against mine as we sat on the stairs; he moved away so we no longer touched.* "And I don't get it, Penelope, because nothing's really changed. I'm the same person, he's the same person—we're just not in school, that's all."

Nick loved to touch me. When we walked together, he rubbed his shoulder against mine or slid his arm around me. He played with my fingers as he held my hand. At school, when we were together but not touching, I felt a force that drew my skin to his, and I could feel a physical tension between us that was almost pleasure.

"Maybe he just needs space," Penelope said.

"He's got tons of space. He lives out in the country; I live in the city. We've never studied together, so I don't see him at night during the week. He's always done his own thing with sports and extracurriculars. That's space, if you ask me."

"Come on, Neela. You know what I'm talking about. Maybe he thinks you're—you know—clinging to him."

"Clinging? Wait a minute. Nick was the one who went after me." I sounded defensive because I couldn't admit my elation that he was the one who'd started calling every night, when we were just friends. He was the one who made tapes of his favorite songs and slipped the

37

cassettes into my backpack. He was the one who'd touched my hand first, who'd kissed me in the school parking lot, who'd given me the nerve to take him up to the third floor.

"Which of you went after the other in the beginning is ancient history, Neela. The point is, now, have you got your arm around his neck?"

I saw us together, my arms around his neck, and his around my waist. But that wasn't what she had in mind. "By that, I guess you mean, am I choking him?"

"Choking. Suffocating. Something like that."

"No, of course not." I tried to sound indignant, but my voice broke with the terror that she might be right.

"It's just an idea, Neela. I'm probably way off base. Forget it."

"Forget it," she had said. "OK," I replied. One word, but my voice sounded flat.

"How do I know what I'm talking about, anyhow?" She got up on her hands and knees. "My only boyfriend has four hoofs and a tail."

I sat up, hands behind my neck, raising myself slowly by my stomach muscles.

Penelope stood, holding out her hand to pull me to my feet. "Come on. It's going to be another month before I see you. Let's go downstairs and get some chocolate cake before my father polishes it off."

Penelope watched me home, as our parents had taught us to do when we were little. Porch lights lit the outside of her house so brightly that, when I turned to wave from mine, she looked like a lone passenger on a ship deck, sailing the dark sea that was Arlington Place. Surely she was going to exotic lands—Vermont seemed that far distant, and one month that long a time.

As I took my key from my shorts pocket, I heard a noise at the end of the block that could have been an elephant trumpeting for a mate, followed by a round of squawks like quarreling crows. I knew the sound well. It was old Mr. Potter staggering back from a bar, bellowing fragments of songs in his drunken way. Penelope and I rarely saw him during the day, but when it became dusk he'd steal out of his house and shuffle down Arlington Place. When we were kids playing soccer in the last moments of light or sitting on our steps in the evening, he'd try to slip by us. We'd call out hello to him. His hand would beat in his pants pocket and then shake up to the brim of the dark felt hat he wore summer and winter. When he was out of earshot, we'd chant "Potter, Potter, teeter-totter." He'd slink through the pedestrian gates at the end of the sidewalk, fumbling endlessly with the padlock and chains, then walk three blocks to a dingy bar that was next to the drugstore Susannah wouldn't let me go to anymore because she said the area was much too seamy.

Quickly I put the key into the front door lock and turned it. I hadn't admitted it even to Penelope, but Mr. Potter scared me. I knew he was harmless—at this time of night it took all his concentration to stay on his feet and howl out a few phrases—but I didn't want to take a chance he'd see me. As soon as I was inside, the heavy front door closed on the elephant sound.

I looked into the living room. The Tiffany lamps were still on, glowing with the muted colors of stained-glass windows. The dogs had been returned to the kennel, and

Susannah and Leonard were in bed, their two empty nightcap glasses on the table.

Upstairs, I sat in front of my glass-topped dressing table from the 1930s, which Susannah had recently re-skirted with a Laura Ashley print she said would make a fetching combination of old and new. My silver-backed brush was part of a vanity set that Susannah had bought and decided to let me keep because each piece happened to be engraved with my initials.

I looked into the mirror and, lifting my hair with the back of my hand, I saw how silky and thick it was, a rich chestnut color. I had it trimmed once a month, so it just skimmed my shoulders and fell into place easily. My eyes were big and dark even without makeup, and I had a cinnamon dusting of freckles across my cheeks. Generally, I liked the way I looked. Why, I wondered, should I ever give another thought to Bertie Albrecht?

Bertie Albrecht. Even the whisper of her name felt like poison in my blood. *Was Nick really at home tonight?* I stared at the telephone on my bedside table. Then I sat cross-legged on my bed, under the safety of the canopy, and put the phone in my lap. I held the receiver to my ear as I dialed Nick's number.

It was late—his mother would be in bed with her phone unplugged, and if Nick were home he'd answer. If he were out, the phone would ring and ring. As I pushed the last digit of his number, my finger went to the plunger and hovered over it. I knew then, I wasn't going to talk to Nick, just find out if he were home.

One ring. I only needed to hear his voice. Two rings. "Hel—"

My finger jammed down the plunger. It was Nick,

his voice heavy with sleep. I could imagine his rumpled look and his sweet, musty breath. My palms tingled with shame. I began to sweat, praying he'd never find out I'd done something so low. *I'll never, never do anything like that again.* I pressed my temples to keep my brain inside my head, and just then I heard a dog howl as Mr. Potter reeled under my open window, bellowing and cawing.

THREE

*N*ick called just as I'd finished stirring artichoke hearts into the pasta sauce.

I'd known how to cook since I was twelve—and not just fudge or brownies or the usual things kids fool around with in the kitchen. I could make entire meals: chicken breasts in wine with tarragon, scalloped potatoes, blueberry pie. Susannah and Leonard liked good food. They would tolerate no mixes on our shelves, no Lean Cuisine in the freezer. They taught me to cook because they said I was an equal partner in this household and had to contribute to the running of it.

I resented cooking when I was younger. Though I didn't complain about it—what good could that do?—I sometimes showed it by burning an omelet or making what I called a "concoction" without a recipe, which would be totally inedible. Susannah would dump these failures in the dog pans and make me start over, *The Joy of Cooking* opened to the proper page. I learned to be grateful for my skills. On the nights I cooked we ate at a decent hour, the same time as my friends, and afterward

I had the evening to study and talk on the phone. When Susannah and Leonard were in charge, dinner often wasn't until nine o'clock.

On the first ring of the phone, I was staring at the little patterns my breath made as I blew into a spoonful of sauce. I'd dumped the spoon and sauce back into the pot and grabbed the receiver by the second ring.

"Neela."

That was all I needed. Nick said my name; he didn't ask it, as though there was any question who I was. He made *Neela* whole and full, like a perfect song made of two notes.

"I've found a job!"

"Fabulous, Nick. Where?"

"Neela Stokes, may I introduce you to Nicholas Cunningham, now employed by Uncle Sam's, the largest—and I mean the biggest and the best—emporium of cassettes, albums, and CDs in Missouri."

"The one in the West County Mall?"

"Yup. A job at last, after three depressing days. Looked like everyone in the city and the county had already hired their summer help. I couldn't believe it when Uncle Sam's said they needed someone."

"That's so great!"

"The only problem is the distance. I can ride my bike over there in half an hour, but the only route is along major roads. It's going to be tough at night."

"What do you mean, 'at night'?"

"Safety. I'm going to have to get a headlight and put more fluorescent tape on my bike."

"Nick, backtrack please. What are your hours going to be?"

"Well, the job's just what I wanted, but it's two days and three nights a week."

"Three nights a week? Three?" My voice cracked, stuck in scratched-record mode again. *He plans to work three nights a week plus play music with Bertie and the new group?*

"Three's not so many." He might have been trying to be reassuring, but he sounded defensive, as though he didn't quite believe himself.

"I don't get it, Nick. A night job? Why did you take it?" I kicked aside the long phone cord that lay tangled at my feet.

"Those were the only hours I could get. And this is really a good summer job. It pays pretty well—and I can't believe how good the sound system is in the store."

"What are you going to be doing there?" *Three nights a week I couldn't see Nick.*

"Stocking shelves."

"Nick, don't you think you're going to get tired of that quickly? Just a few days ago you said you wanted something challenging." That sounded like a phrase Susannah or Leonard would use.

"No I didn't, I just said I didn't want to be bored. This is going to be OK."

I used the few seconds of silence to try to erase the disappointment and disapproval from my voice. I wanted to stop being my parents and be the me Nick loved, but it was hard. "Well, you sound pretty up about it all." That was the best I could manage.

"Why not? Listen. Uncle Sam—the dude who runs the place—what a character! He struts around the store with red and white striped pants held up by blue suspenders. Anyway—though I'm just stocking shelves to begin with—he said when I get to know the inventory he's going to put me on the sales staff. That's two bucks more an hour."

"Great," I said, but I knew I didn't sound enthusiastic. Uncle Sam's—the place that advertised on the radio: "*What a value! What a deal! Rock 'n' roll with sex appeal!*" So Nick was going to be on the sales staff—the sex appeal.

"And there's a bonus—a big employees' discount. Not only am I going to have the most awesome cassette collection by the end of the summer, but I can get tapes for you and the rest of my friends."

The rest of his friends. He lumped me in with his friends.

"I start tomorrow morning, so I don't have to work tomorrow night. That means we can do something." For the last three days, while he'd been out on his bike looking for a job, he'd been too depressed and tired in the evenings to go out. Or so he'd said. "Tomorrow?" I asked, and I could hear my voice still edged with suspicion.

"Are you busy? Have you got something else going?"

"Not really. Not anything I can't change."

"We're on, then." He waited for me to say something, but I couldn't, because all I was thinking was *Why not tonight?* He cleared his throat. "So what's happening over there?"

"Just catching up on a lot of stuff." I hunched my shoulder to anchor the receiver to my ear, while I picked up the phone and untangled the long cord, as though it were a chore that needed doing.

"Like?"

"You know, the usual. Cooking." Tormenting ideas

buzzed around me like mosquitoes. *Evenings. Sex appeal. The rest of my friends.*

"Cooking what?" *Was he trying to extend this conversation because he really wanted to talk to me, or was he trying to make up for not seeing me?*

"Sauce for pasta."

"Whoa, you sound just like your folks. In my house *pasta* is still *spaghetti*."

"You know Susannah, she's the queen of proper terminology." I tried to sound nonchalant, as though everyone had a mother like mine. "She says pasta is generic. When she gets specific she's talking *capellini* or *fettuccine*."

"Whatever. Look, my mom's coming home from work soon, and I want to give her the good news about my job. But I wanted to tell you first, so I called you from a phone booth. Pick me up at six-thirty tomorrow night, right?"

"Right. I love you, Nick." I let it out in one breath, the phrase I held back so often. It seemed I only told Nick I loved him when we were getting passionate or when I was apologizing for something—even if I didn't know what it was. When things were good between us, I didn't need to tell him I loved him. He knew it.

"You too, Neela."

We hung up. I hadn't asked what he was going to do tonight. *Clinging*, Penelope had said. I didn't want to be the kind of dreary person who was all over her boyfriend. But for some reason, this summer—which even last week had seemed like it would be the best time of my life—now looked empty and lonely. It felt like a *nothing* time. I had to break out of it. I turned off the flame under the pasta sauce. *Spaghetti* sauce.

So I called Susan Margolis. Her sister said she'd gone

to Ohio to look at colleges with her mother. I called Janice Oldenbach, but got only an answering machine that was sorry, no one could come to the phone right now. I called the Hereford twins—who insisted their surname had nothing to do with cows—but they'd left for camp the same day Penelope had. I couldn't find one good friend around.

And Penelope—this was missing her. This was wanting to run down the block, and slam the door to her room and scream: *How have I let myself get so knotted up in Nick? How can his mood, his words, his life affect me as though they were my own? Why do I go nuts when I hear that he has to work three nights a week? Why has music become a code word for Bertie Albrecht? Help me, Penelope, make me laugh at myself.*

I froze when I heard the dogs start to snarl. Onions barked out the chant, throaty and mean: *kill, kill, kill.* Liver threw himself against the chain-link kennel with a smashing noise like an over-miked cymbal. Susannah had been very clear: no deliveries were due today, and under no circumstances was I to allow anyone in the house. But the dogs were equally clear: Someone was at the back door.

I slid the thick brass chain into the door plate before I peeked outside. The sun bouncing off the limestone gravel of the dog-exercise area—our former grass back-yard—made it look like the washed-out, white background of a home movie. In the foreground, on the wooden back steps, was an old lady.

"Open up, Neela," Aunt Amelia called. Her voice sounded hoarse and a little frightened. "I forgot my key."

When I shut the door to unclasp the chain, she must

have thought I was going to lock her out again. Her voice spiraled up desperately against the barking. "It's me, it's me, Amelia!"

I knocked back the chain and yanked open the door. Then I got a good look at her. She wore a black, long-sleeved dress that must have held the heat like the solid, old furnace in our basement. Moisture dotted her forehead, above pencil-drawn, fernlike eyebrows. Her white wispy hair had separated into strings where clear plastic combs pulled it up from her face and neck. She sported silver dangle earrings almost to her shoulders.

"You scared me, Aunt Amelia."

"I didn't scare you, the hounds did." She turned and glared out at the dogs. "Be quiet!" she yelled, with more volume than I thought her shaky, old woman's voice could muster, and to my amazement they fell silent.

"Thank you for letting me in." The *thank you* sounded reluctant, as though she were a debater conceding a point. "I thought I might find the back door unlocked and be able to get in without a fuss, but I forgot about the dogs."

"No problem, Aunt Amelia." I was surprised to find myself so amiable, but the truth was, I felt glad to see her. First, she hadn't been the knife-wielding mugger I half expected to find; and second, I needed someone to talk to right now. I didn't need an intimate conversation, but I needed to hear normal words come from my mouth. "Let me give you a hand with your stuff." Two large shopping bags were clenched in her arms.

"I can manage," she said, quite curtly. She tried to peer over the top of her bags, while using one foot—as a blind person might use a cane—to find the step that would bring her up over the threshold.

I held the door while she shuffled through the kitchen into the front hall. She heaved her bags onto the big oak table, then rolled and stretched her shoulders while her breath came in short, rasping little puffs.

"Oh, help!" she suddenly cried. One of the shopping bags collapsed onto its side, the contents shifting and settling like an old, arthritic dog lying down. I grabbed the bags to keep the things inside from spilling.

"Gracious," she cried. "Don't let those bottles fall out. They're full of chemicals." She jammed her purse against the bag, while I pushed jars and cans and bottles back in. "Broken glass on this antique table—potassium ferrocyanide on Susannah's Persian rug—never!"

I snickered without looking at her. *Imagine Susannah coming home to such a mess.* "It's okay, Aunt Amelia, I've got it."

"You're sure?" A bead of moisture trickled down her forehead as she slowly withdrew the purse.

I propped up the shopping bag, which had the large red-and-yellow KODAK logo on it. "What is all this stuff?"

"Darkroom chemicals."

"For what?"

"For me."

I had no idea what she meant. I knew, of course, that darkroom chemicals had to do with photography. There was a small darkroom next to *The Guardian* office for the photo staff to use.

"I'm going upstairs now," she announced. As she pulled one of the bags by its handle, she knocked it into Susannah's silver plate. The business cards bounced like fifty-two card pick-up onto the rug. I crouched down and started to retrieve them. "Oh dear, I'm making a real mess of things today," she moaned. I glanced up to find Aunt Amelia's eyes squeezed shut, her fingers spread across her face as though she were trying to hide behind the branches of a knotty old tree.

"It's no big deal." In fact, it felt good to have someone in this house making a mess of things. I rearranged Susannah's cards in two neat piles on the silver tray, swung one shopping bag off the table, picked up the other bag, and started for the stairs.

"Where are you going with my things?" she asked sharply.

"I'm taking them up to the third floor."

"You mean to my apartment?"

I almost unlocked my fingers and let the bags crash. I wanted to see the plastic rip, the bottles break, the chemicals spread across the floor. This mean, ungrateful great-aunt had not only taken over my secret place, now she was demanding I refer to it as "her apartment." But I knew too well from Leonard and Susannah that saying something *snippy*—their word—just made things worse.

At the top of the stairs, I set down the shopping bags in front of her door. Because she was tall, she didn't have to stand on tiptoe to find her door key above the transom, and after just a few seconds of groping, she had it in her hand. I stood with folded arms, watching as she put it in the lock. She didn't fumble, as I thought an old lady might, but inserted the key and turned it with the authority of someone for whom mechanical things came easily. Suddenly, I could imagine her fixing bikes or changing headlights.

"This is for you," she said, as she handed me a dollar.

"What for?"

"Carrying my bags, of course."

"Aunt Amelia, I carried these things up because I wanted to." I wasn't a mover delivering furniture: I was her relative.

"Well now, aren't you a well-bred, polite child. Humm. What to do with a girl like you? Couldn't you use a dollar?"

I shook my head. "Susannah's at an auction today. She's paying me to take care of the house when she goes out."

"All right then, if I can't give you money, how about a glass of lemonade?"

"I don't know," I said hesitantly. I was torn. I wanted to flee downstairs and get away from her crankiness, but I also wanted to see in detail what my third floor hide-away had turned into. "I really should . . ."

"As you will. It's up to you. We all make choices."

"OK. Lemonade."

I was past the door, inside my magic rooms. Because I'd peeked in the one time I'd been here before, I knew how changed everything was, but I hadn't expected to find that while everything looked different, the feeling of the place could still be the same. I walked to the dormer window of her sitting room—that's how I thought of it, since our big downstairs room was a living room—and remembered how I could perch on the wide sill for hours, my knees pulled up to my chest, looking out into the shiny leaves of our huge magnolia tree.

"A nice place to sit, don't you think?" Her voice had turned wistful, muted.

How did she know?

"I'm thinking of having a cushion made to turn it into

a proper window seat. Sitting in the window is like being part of that tree."

I didn't say anything. But that was exactly the way I felt.

"I grew up in this house, you know. Or didn't Leonard tell you?" She cocked her head to the side as though she expected me to answer, but even if I'd planned to, she didn't give me time. "This room was special to me when I was a child. Mother declared the third floor off limits because the couple who worked for us lived here, but Hilda—the maid—used to let me come up after school with my pens and watercolors. I'd sit on that windowsill for hours with my sketch pad."

"I used to come up here, too," I said.

"I had a feeling you had some connection to these rooms."

"But they were all shabby and dusty." I looked around at the polished wood floor and the cool, white walls. I ran my hand over the soft leather couch. "It's so different now."

"And when you used this room it was different from the way it was when I came up here. Hilda and her husband only had a couple of ugly stuffed chairs and a round oak table, and yet it always seemed the nicest place in the house to me."

I glanced over at Aunt Amelia. I wondered if she was really unhappy all the time. Deep crevices ran from her nostrils to the corners of her mouth, making it seem as though her whole face were flowing downhill.

"And it still does seem the nicest place in the house," she continued after a pause. "Come, I'll show you some of the other changes I've made."

The bedroom had only a single bed, covered with a zigzag patterned Indian blanket so it looked like a couch with throw pillows on it. The green steel desk under the window was bare except for a mug full of pencils and a goose-neck lamp. Everything was spare and orderly. But in the corner by the door stood an ungainly stack of perhaps a dozen gray flat boxes, each piled in precarious balance on another. The top one was open, and in it I could see a large black-and-white photograph. It was mounted on cream-colored poster board, just as we mounted art work at school for shows; the photograph itself was veiled by a delicate overlay of tissue paper.

"What's in all these boxes?" I asked, pointing.

"Those are my portfolios."

"That means pictures? Can I see some?"

"Move along, move along." As she shooed me out, I tried to catch a look at the photograph again, but she shut the door behind me.

The bathroom fixtures had all been replaced and were modern and anonymous; I missed the turquoise-green stained sink. The kitchen, which had once been good sized, was now as small as a ship's galley and just as tidy, with everything behind closed doors. It still smelled of new paint, as though nothing had yet been cooked in it.

She opened a small refrigerator door and pulled out a glass pitcher—like Leonard's martini pitcher—half full of lemonade. When she opened a cabinet for glasses, I saw it was almost empty.

"I don't have many belongings anymore," she said. "When I left New York, after Oliver died, I sold everything. I didn't want the same china and crystal and silver we'd shared for so many, many years to be mine alone."

"Oliver was your husband?" I asked that just to fill the pause.

"Oh yes, he was indeed. We worked side by side for forty-five years."

I wanted to know when Oliver died. I wanted to know what kind of work they did. I wanted to know what it was like living in New York. Instead I heard myself ask how old she was when she met Oliver.

"How old? About your age, I'd guess. Or perhaps a year or two older. I met him my first week of college."

I still had more than a year before I went to college: A fall of college tours and interviews; a winter of essays and application deadlines; a spring waiting to find out if I was acceptable.

"Did you ever . . ." I hesitated, wondering if this was the kind of question you asked someone you barely knew.

"Did I ever what?"

"Bring him up here?" I continued. "I mean, when you were in college, did he ever see this third floor?" Now I was dangerously close to Nick.

"Oh my, yes." Then for the first time she smiled and her cheeks pushed up, reversing the downward movement of lines around her mouth and eyes. "The Christmas of our junior year, Oliver came to St. Louis to spend the holidays with me. It was after the Depression, and we couldn't afford to have a couple working for us any longer, so Hilda and her husband had to depart for a fancier house and wealthier people. These third-floor rooms were vacant. Oliver and I would wait until Mother and Father were soundly sleeping, then we'd sneak up these stairs. Oh yes, he knew this place well."

And all the time I was thinking *Nick, Nick, Nick*. We'd

been up here too, only Susannah and Leonard weren't sleeping, they were out at dinner parties, and Nick and I would lie on the mattress that Susannah never sold because it was just old, not antique, and I would make up stories for him about the other people who had been here, and then after a while he would kiss me. He would kiss me, his hands warming my body where they touched me under my clothes, and then my insides melted, and a heated feeling spread through my belly and hips.

"Why child, I do believe you know what I'm talking about." Aunt Amelia was squinting at me, trying to see clearer through black mascara lashes.

I turned my back so she wouldn't see the tears I felt begin behind my eyes. If I could concentrate on her and not Nick, there wouldn't be anxiety in my voice. "Not really, Aunt Amelia," I lied.

"Perhaps you have some young man in your life."

I couldn't talk about Nick. I had to get out of this conversation; I had to find a way back into being a normal person. We could chat about anything else—weather, lemonade, dogs, anything.

"So," I began, my voice chipper. "Isn't this kitchen a lot smaller than it used to be?"

She tossed her head as though she were shaking off a dream, and her tone went back to the clipped, no-nonsense way she usually spoke. "Correct. It's half the size."

"What happened to the rest?"

"Retrieve those packages from the sitting room and I'll show you," she said.

I did as she told me, and when I returned she was standing next to the kitchen entrance, in front of a closed door. As she turned the knob she took a deep breath, as though it were a door she was afraid to open.

I looked into a long, narrow laboratory. A formica counter and a stainless steel sink ran along one wall; on a shelf above the sink were brown glass bottles of various sizes and several accordion-pleated containers. The other long wall was also lined with a counter, this one holding two formidable machines—columns of steel reaching to the ceiling, with thick coiled wires, and ratchets, and dome-shaped tops.

"You see, of course, what I've done," Aunt Amelia declared. "Cut the kitchen in half to make a darkroom."

This was not like *The Guardian* darkroom, a small and cluttered space that always smelled of some pungent chemical mixed with forbidden, stale cigarette smoke. This room was clean and sleek, and yet somehow cozy —perhaps because its narrowness made it the perfect size for one or two people. You could stand at the sink and turn around to the machines by pivoting without having to take more than a step.

"What do you need a darkroom for, Aunt Amelia?" As I said that, I remembered the boxes piled in the bedroom. But I hadn't seen any photographs on her apartment walls—in fact, they were bare, all painted the same icy white.

She looked at me in disbelief, her arms firmly crossed and creases forming between her penciled eyebrows. "I've been a photographer for forty-five years, my dear. That's why I need it."

"I didn't know that."

"I guess my nephew hasn't filled you in on much about your great-aunt. And I suppose that, if I'm honest, my past isn't very important. Right now I'm not making any new photographs, and I'm not using this darkroom, and that's that."

"Why not?" My questions seemed more direct than ones I would usually ask. With Susannah and Leonard I'd learned to keep conversation tidy, so it wouldn't slip into difficult areas.

"Because Oliver's dead, that's why. And it's like the china and the glasses and the rest of my belongings: I don't want anything that we had together to be mine alone."

Suddenly I became aware that I was still holding the shopping bags, one in each hand. "Why did you buy all this new stuff, then?" I asked, putting the bags on the counter.

"Because you never know. That's how I feel today, but tomorrow could be another story. And I must admit I miss the daily routine of my old life, so I thought I'd at least locate a good photo store and replenish my supplies, just in case."

Just in case. Nick came back to me again then, his face filling my thoughts and blocking out Aunt Amelia's voice. Whatever she said from then on was lost, because I was lost, thinking of Nick. I should go downstairs and be near the phone *just in case* he called. I should wash my hair, *just in case* he changed his mind and I could somehow see him tonight.

He didn't call, and I didn't see him that night, but at six-thirty the next evening, as we'd planned, I picked Nick up at his house. Since he was such an ardent cyclist, he'd never seriously considered owning a car, and in the

57

nine months we'd been together he said he hadn't thought about it at all because I had the glorious little VW Bug. He'd gotten his license when he was sixteen like everyone else—because that's what you were supposed to do— but he could get anywhere he needed during the day on his bike, and the nighttime driving he left to me. Some people thought it was wimpy to have a girl drive you around, but no one thought Nick Cunningham was a wimp. I actually liked driving, and I liked picking him up; somehow, it gave me a feeling of power.

Nick's mom opened the door, looking terrific in blue nylon racing shorts and a purple tank top that showed off her strong shoulders and firm, tough arms. There was nothing hanging or flapping anywhere on Mrs. Cunningham. Her forehead glistened under the sweatband that stretched across her brow and caught her curly hair in back, pulling it up off her neck.

"Well, look who it is, at last. Hi there, Neela." She gave me a sweaty little hug, carefully keeping her body away, but letting her moist cheek rub against mine.

"Fabulous new running shoes," I said, admiring her pristine white sneakers with the silver lightning bolt on the side.

"Yup, the latest in technology. The shoes are supposed to have air inside which somehow guarantees that I'll run twice as fast. Come on in. Nick's upstairs."

Mrs. Cunningham was cool, even though she was a maniac athlete. She worked all day as a physical therapist in a hospital, then came home and ran five miles, or went to her gym for hours. She liked to take Nick on vigorous vacations—skiing in Colorado, or hiking in the Ozarks, or even, once, two weeks in a New Hampshire rowing camp learning to scull.

Nick and I were both only children. But that was the single similarity in our backgrounds. Susannah and Leonard never had another kid because they didn't want one. I used to beg them for a brother or sister, but they wouldn't even consider it. They said we were a perfect trio. Nick's father had disappeared when he was a baby, so it had been just Nick and his mom as long as he could remember.

There was no way we could compare our mothers, they were so different. Susannah, for instance, never exercised, although she always talked about how she wanted to. Last year she actually started taking a ballet class, and to my dismay began practicing in my bedroom, clutching the post of my canopy bed for balance. But that only lasted for a few weeks, and then she was back to the only exercise she really did well—shuffling furniture.

Mrs. Cunningham was an easygoing person who believed Nick's room was his private domain and allowed him to have me in there with the door shut. She also let him crank the stereo and was going to let him fix up the garage as a place for the new rock group to practice. Susannah definitely would have called her "permissive." I was glad they'd never met.

I didn't bother to knock on Nick's door, since he couldn't have heard a jet plane through the incredible volume of the Stones. His back was to me when I entered, so I had as long as I wanted to take in the scene.

Nick had hung our maroon-and-blue felt school banner over one window and tacked up a tie-dyed sheet over the other, so his room was as dark as a cave. Posters of some of the living and dead greats of rock 'n' roll hung on his wall like giant bats—Chuck Berry, Led Zeppelin,

Jimi Hendrix, Pete Townshend, Eddie Van Halen, Peter Gabriel, and Jerry Garcia—of course. The buttons and dials of his stereo gleamed from the black stack of tape deck, receiver, amplifier, turntable, and CD player in the corner, and two enormous speakers faced the door. Because his room was air-conditioned, he had a winter quilt on his bed which was supposed to serve as a bedspread and make everything look neat, but tonight, as always, it had slipped off and was bunched on the floor.

He sat on a stool, bent over his guitar, and I had to tap him on the shoulder to get his attention. What I really wanted to do was kiss the back of his neck, but it seemed like a bit of an overwhelming way to say hello. He swung around, still running a hand up the guitar neck, and I could tell he wasn't saying *hi* yet, but was still mouthing the words to "Honky-Tonk Woman," shrieking to a climax on the stereo. He shaped his mouth into a fat Mick Jagger sneer as the song ended, then winked at me.

"Hey, woman, what are you doing here?" he said in a gruff, bass voice not his own.

"OK, buddy, don't get into that sexist stuff just because you're listening to the Stones." The next tune blared on, cutting me off, so I turned down the volume. "And could we please lower the decibel level?" My words rang out in total disharmony with the way I wanted to start this evening.

"And miss 'Sympathy for the Devil'? No way." He rolled the volume up with his thumb.

"Nick," I screeched, but it didn't come out positive and strong; it was drawn out—"Ni-ick,"—and a little whiny.

"OK, I'm just giving you a hard time." He swung

the guitar onto the bed and came over to me. He touched my face, running his hand up from the corner of my mouth, trying to draw it into a smile.

It worked. Having Nick's hands on me, any way, always made me feel good. I carefully slid his guitar to the end of his bed, sat down, and leaned back against a fat corduroy-covered pillow. "So where do you want to go tonight? I've got the paper with the movie listings in the car."

"I thought we could just stay here."

"Great," I said—a small word for the enormous happiness I felt. Everything expanded inside me, as though I were smiling from the inside out. I plumped up another pillow next to me for Nick.

"Not really here, as in *right here*," he said gesturing around the room.

"Here, but not here?" I asked, covering the same territory with my eyes. "So then, where?"

"Well, I asked the new band to come over. We kind of wanted to get started fixing up the garage so we'd have a place to practice. If you help, and everyone pitches in, it'll only take a few hours."

I felt the stun of hurt all over me, as though I'd been sprayed with little shotgun pellets. Then it fused into one rifle bullet in my stomach. And the pain made me angry. "Wait a minute, Nick. This is our time together. You and I had a date."

"I know, but with my new job I just can't do it all. Come on, Neela, give me a break."

I could see by the way he drew into himself that he was angry, too. I wanted to stand up for myself. But as always, my indignation turned to tears. And crying was unacceptable. Not to mention, as Leonard would point out, that it was terribly unattractive.

"Come on, don't do that," Nick whispered when he saw tears forming in my eyes. "It's no big deal. We have lots of time this summer."

"But you just said you didn't have any time."

"Right now. It's just for right now. Things will change." He knelt next to me and took my chin in his hand. "Let's do this with the band tonight, and we can go to the movies or wherever you want another night soon."

"Promise?" I felt like a two-year-old.

"Promise. Now cheer up, 'cause they're due any time."

The tape on the stereo had finished, and there was silence in the room as Nick kissed me, his lips brushing against mine, and then pressing with the same love I'd felt since we began seeing each other. But as we came apart, and I looked at him—wanting *more, more, more* with every bit of my body and heart—there was a knock on the door. Without waiting for a response from Nick, the knob turned, and two guys I'd never seen before walked into the room, followed by none other than Bertie Albrecht.

FOUR

Weekday mornings, Leonard looked crisp
and ready for business when he came into the kitchen.
His brown, English-made shoes gleamed with the soft
luster of daily buffing, his pants had a sharp crease, and
a perky bow tie defined the edges of his starched collar.
Faint fold lines showed on his shirts, from the cardboard
stiffener which the Just Right! dry cleaners slipped inside. I used to beg Leonard to save the cardboard for me
to draw on, because I loved the way magic marker colors
became dense and vivid on the creamy, polished surface;
some mornings he would come downstairs waving one,
and other mornings he wouldn't, and later I'd find the
cardboard ripped in two in his wastebasket.

"Good morning, Neela, my dear." He sauntered into
the kitchen carrying his suit jacket, which he arranged
—smoothing the shoulders and straightening the lapels
—on the back of a kitchen chair. I sat slumped at the
butcher-block table. As he scratched the top of my head,
I caught a whiff of lavender after-shave. In his brisk voice
was none of the fatigue and anger I heard at night: He

had been renewed. I was always startled—yet grateful—that he could put yesterday behind him and get on with today, no matter how worked-up he'd been the night before because I'd come home too late, nor how long he and Susannah had squabbled in their bedroom. What worried me was that even though today started well, it would usually end up like yesterday.

Unlike our evening exchanges, when Leonard dragged home too bushed to speak, it was I who muttered hello this morning and kept my eyes on the newspaper. Leonard moved around in the kitchen, opening cabinets, peering into the refrigerator, and measuring coffee for the old glass percolator (no plastic coffee maker in our kitchen).

"Caramel roll, Neela?" he asked, chipper as a robin.

"Uh-uhn."

"Excuse me. What?"

"No thanks. No breakfast."

"Neela, you must eat. You'll blow away on the next wind."

"Hardly," I snorted. I leaned my head in my hand and hunched down farther over the paper, to prove how vitally interested I was in the front page. Actually, plane crashes, hostages, robberies, murders—they were all the same to me. My world had shrunk to fourteen letters that spelled Bertie Albrecht.

From their kennel, Liver, Bacon, and Onions must have seen Leonard pass in front of the window, or perhaps a hint of his after-shave had drifted outside, or maybe they'd heard a trace of his voice: whatever, it set them to howling and baying and whimpering.

Leonard yanked open the back door. "All right. I

want all you dogs to be quiet out there and I mean it!"
His shouting pierced the morning like an alarm clock. I
imagined the neighborhood bolting up in their beds.

The aroma of coffee overwhelmed the smell of brown-
ing caramel rolls as Leonard poured two cups, one for
each of us. Pouring was always the best part of the morning ritual. The worst came in a few minutes, when the
coffee was cool enough to drink. Breakfast was his culinary area of expertise, and he insisted each morning
should begin with a good, strong cup of coffee.

"Cheers," he said, holding his cup above the saucer
and nodding to me.

"Cheers," I replied, doing the same, although cheer
seemed no longer in my vocabulary. Leonard kept his
eyes on me as I lifted the cup to my mouth and drank.
No milk, no sugar was allowed, lest the purity of the
taste be compromised. So I sipped the coffee as though
it were terribly hot, trying to draw in as much air as
liquid through pursed lips. It tasted bitter and gritty. It
felt like swamp mud.

"Hits the spot, no?"

"Hits the spot," I echoed.

"Puts hair on your chest," he said with satisfaction.

I resisted the urge to run my hand inside my shirt.
Instead, I returned to staring at the headlines. Leonard
rushed back to the toaster-oven as a thin plume of smoke
signaled that melted sugar from the caramel rolls was
burning on the coils.

"Damn," he exploded.

"Sorry," I said.

When he'd rescued his breakfast, he could sit at the
butcher-block table for the next twenty minutes with the

sports page and the financial section, so absorbed he never noticed that I didn't touch my coffee again. I wouldn't have to leave the room to be alone with my thoughts.

Bertie Albrecht. From the moment she walked into Nick's room, three nights ago, I realized the ideas Penelope and I had about her were all wrong. *How could I have been so deluded?*

Her hair wasn't stringy at all; long and straight, a little thin, yes, but it hung together like a curtain, sweeping over her shoulders and down her back. Somehow it wasn't the mousy beige I'd remembered either—perhaps she'd been hitting the peroxide bottle—but a soft blonde, with copper highlights. Nor did she wear odd, granola-bar clothes. If anything she veered the other way, trying a little too hard to be chic in her oversized HARD ROCK CAFE—*Honolulu* T-shirt. She slipped out of her klutzy Birkenstocks as soon as she entered Nick's room, as though she were Japanese, and padded across the room wearing nothing on her feet but electric-blue toenails.

"Hey, Neela," she said, deliberately ignoring Nick, as though she'd seen him only five minutes before. She walked right over to the bed, her eyes fixed on me as Leonard's had been, as he waited for me to drink the coffee. "How's the summer going?" *As though we were friends; as though we had lots in common.* I hated her familiarity. I hated that she seemed so comfortable, so at home, in Nick's room.

"Pretty good, Bertie." I emphasized *good*. "How about yours?"

"Excellent."

"What are you up to?" As soon as I asked I knew it

was a mistake. If there was one thing I didn't want to hear, it was how the summer was perfect because she was singing with this group.

"I still can hardly believe it, but I'm a lifeguard at the Crestwood pool."

"Oh yeah?" I let my eyes flick from her face and dart over to Nick. He'd gotten up from the bed and was flipping through some cassettes by the stereo. He was paying no attention to us. "How did you manage a job like that?"

Bertie tucked her hair behind her ears, showing off big silver hoop earrings, and then stroked her temples. "It took a lot of work. I had to get my senior life-saving certificate and start interviewing last March."

I took a breath to say, "How nice," in a cool, dismissive way, but Bertie plunged right on.

"Of course I already had my Red Cross first aid, and I took a CPR course over the winter, because I knew that would help my chances."

"How nice," I said at last.

"And I've been on the swim team for three years," she continued undaunted. "That counts for something on your resumé."

Bertie made landing a lifeguard job sound as prestigious as getting into Harvard. From my vantage point, it was. Lifeguarding might actually be just a police job, blowing whistles and yelling at kids, but all I could fantasize was the glamor—Bertie spending days in the sun, oiling up her skin and showing off her body.

"And then there's this band." Bertie's face turned pink, the color inching up her jawline to her ears.

Here we go.

"I'm a little nervous about it."

"Why?" I drew out the word, my tone incredulous, as though I was saying, *How could anyone be the tiniest bit nervous about such a simple thing?* I also heard how cruel I'd managed to make that one word sound. When I looked at Bertie's face, stung by my attitude into slack insecurity, I knew I had won. *Some victory.* I felt awful.

There was a terrible pause while we both wrestled with what to say next. It was obvious we had to change the subject, but there seemed to be nowhere safe for it to go. I couldn't give her a chance to ask what I was doing: *Oh, answering the phone and baby-sitting my mother's antiques.*

"I'm involved in some independent projects this summer, myself," I announced. I glanced furtively at Nick to see if he'd overheard me and, mercifully, it was just at the moment he was trying to get the band's attention.

"Hey, guys—let's mobilize to the garage and start working." He flicked the overhead light on and off, opened his bedroom door, and stood there waiting for us to file out. "Come on, let's get cranking." The band swept through the door first, still without a word to me. Bertie followed, jamming her feet into her clumsy leather sandals and clunking down the stairs. As I passed by Nick, who still held the door, I felt his hand on the small of my back, either hurrying me along or giving me an affectionate pat, I couldn't tell which.

Leonard pushed the paper away in disgust, swiped at his mouth with his napkin, and prepared to leave for work. The Cards had lost last night and the national debt was continuing to rise. It seemed as though each minute that took him further from his bed further soured his day. He put on his suit jacket without a word to me and left the kitchen muttering about incompetent outfielders and a national policy of fiscal irresponsibility. I heard footsteps as he went upstairs to wake Susannah and kiss her good-bye, then a few minutes later the front door banged closed. The dogs, who seemed to sense Leonard's every move and sometimes mourned his departure with a howl or two, were silent. Now I could stop pretending to read the paper. I could obsess about the rest of that evening, and how it ended the way it did.

Nick's house was the oldest on Willow Lane, the original farmhouse of a sizable tract of land which had been cut into three-acre parcels a long time ago. The newer houses in the suburb were larger and more elegant—most had swimming pools—but his had a casual, old look to it. Everyone felt at home at Nick's. Though Mrs. Cunningham was a fanatic gardener, her flower beds weren't fussy but grew all sorts of things in an overcrowded, luscious way. On Arlington Place the flowers were low, discreet, edging the walkways, but at the Cunninghams' bushes grew high and wild, and flowers got so tall they drooped over.

Behind the house was a garage that looked like a little cottage, made of the same white-painted wood as the house, but camouflaged by vines that clung to the clapboards. The gravel driveway looped around the rear, so the garage door opened toward the wooded back lot, and two ivy-curtained windows faced the house. The garage was further isolated by a fat, leafy hedge that surrounded it. Mrs. Cunningham never seemed to use the garage.

She always parked her car in the turn-out next to the kitchen door. The garage was very private, and perfect for the band.

"This place is going to be awesome, dude," the keyboard player said, looking around.

"You got enough outlets here?" asked the drummer. "We got a lot of stuff to plug in."

"No problem," Nick said. "Someone used it as a shop, once. There's tons of outlets."

"Who used it?" I asked.

"Guess," Nick said. He shot out a bullet of a look, so deadly I had to duck my head.

One night last winter, when his mom was out, Nick had told me what he knew about his father. We'd been sitting on the living-room rug in front of the fire, drinking hot chocolate with marshmallows as though we were kids. It had been snowing, so our boots were in the vestibule, and we sat facing each other, knees drawn up and locked by our arms. The soles of his feet covered the top of my toes to warm them. It was one of those nights when, although we were barely touching, we couldn't have gotten closer.

He told me his parents had met and married in California. His mom wanted to come back to St. Louis, and his dad had agreed to try living here, even though he didn't know anyone, and he didn't know what he wanted to do with his life. Nick described him as kind of a biker—not a heavy-duty Harley type with tattoos and an earring, but more like a nomad. He became sort of a motorcycle mechanic, and one night, when Nick was less than a year old, he took off on a Suzuki he was fixing, and that was that. Nick had asked his mom if they'd been

70

fighting, and she said no, he was just too restless to settle down.

Guess. Nick's father worked on bikes in that garage. That's why Mrs. Cunningham never used it.

Dark oil patches stained the cement floor, the edges indistinct because they'd been made so long ago.

"That's some wallpaper, man," the keyboard player said, still looking around in wonder. He hiked up his shirt and scratched a concave belly.

"It's not wallpaper; that's insulation." Nick nodded proudly at the silver foil with blue printing that lined the interior of the garage. "I've been insulating the place in my spare time. It'll keep the noise down this summer and we can practice in here all winter with an electric heater."

"We ran out of it over there," Bertie added, pointing to a corner where the bare wood still showed, "but Nick's going to finish up tomorrow."

We ran out.

"There's some old stuff down in our basement we can use to make this place more comfortable," Nick said. "Let's go get it."

I wanted time—even a few seconds—alone with Nick. But he sprinted across the lawn to the house. I longed to linger behind on the basement steps with him, just so the band could see that we were a couple, but he stayed ahead of me.

For the next hour we moved furniture. Thanks to Susannah's training, I was good at that and directed the guys in turning corners with the old couch so they could ease it up the basement stairs and outside. The furniture was indeed "stuff"—a couple of armchairs with broken legs, a coffee table so scratched it looked as though some-one had learned to tap-dance on it, a lamp made out of a bottle with a torn shade. Susannah would have died—not an antique in the place.

While we were moving I found out the keyboard player's name—Ronnie. He was the skinniest person I've ever seen, with ribs that poked through his shirt like the springs on the couch we were moving. He told me the drummer was named Bob, but liked to be called Wolf Man.

Bertie didn't move furniture but cleaned up the garage while we made trips back and forth. She swatted cobwebs off the ceiling with a broom and swept the floor. When we came one time she was gone, but by the next trip she was back with a few straw beach mats, which she arranged over the oil spills.

When the furniture was in, the guys brought out their equipment. Wolf Man put together his huge drum set of cymbals and tom-toms, a snare drum, and a deep bass drum. Ronnie's synthesizer had control settings for attack rates and frequency levels, all hi-tech jumble which he explained to me in a low, sincere voice. My nonmathematical, nonscientific mind couldn't get behind the concept of mixers and modulators, much less oscillators and controllers—so he let me play chopsticks on the keyboard.

Nick plugged his Les Paul Sunburst—which he'd spent all last summer working to buy—into the amplifier. He positioned two huge, black speakers toward the audience—me, on the couch. Then he plugged in a mike with a long cord and cradled it in a mike stand. *Bertie's mike*.

The four of them were repositioning instruments; chords and scales came from the speakers; the drum crashed and boomed; and it didn't matter who else was there, or what else was happening: I could not take my eyes off Nick. I sat staring at him.

"Yo, Ronnie!" He tightened the pegs on his guitar, tuning it, running his fingers up and down the frets. "Run a G scale by me." A few seconds later he turned around to joke with Wolf Man. He danced a few steps, his knees like rubber, feet spinning him around. He looked wonderful, at ease, in charge, the man who could do anything.

"OK guys, time for a sound check." Nick tapped the mike with his fingers, and a crackly, spitting noise popped from the speakers. "Let's hear if those skins are in balance, Wolf. All *right*! You got it. Now it's your turn Ronnie." A few chords thundered from the speakers. "Bertie? You're up next. Come on over and do a few notes for us."

"No way, Nick. I'm not going to sing without backup." Her arms were crossed over her chest, hugging her shoulders.

Nick froze for a second. I knew that kind of coyness went no place with him. It was another moment of triumph for me.

"Oh you shy little girl, you." He smiled at Bertie. "OK, later." He leaned into the mike, his lips almost up against it. "Testing two-three-four, testing."

From the center of the garage, Nick gazed out at the couch, and it was almost as though he were on stage, looking over the heads of his audience. I waited for his eyes to come down, to rest on mine. I waited for Nick to smile at me, the same way he'd smiled at Bertie. I waited for a wink, a nod, a shrug, anything.

"Bertie?" he called, pivoting around. "We've got to make sure this is set up right. Go sit on the couch and tell me how it sounds." He leaned toward the mike again. "Testing two-three-four."

I had been on the couch for twenty minutes, his girlfriend, his fan, his helper.

I could hear Susannah coming downstairs, her heels slap, slap, slapping against the soles of her green satin, open-backed slippers. It was the slow, reluctant sound of someone being dragged into the day. She yawned her way into the kitchen dressed in the bathrobe she wore every morning, a body-bouquet of droopy roses with huge, lazy petals.

I never tried to speak to her before she'd had some coffee. Leonard's bog brew had been thickening over low heat on the stove for nearly an hour. I made sure the paper was folded neatly on the table, with a thick, red marker pen next to it. Susannah took a single slice of ultra-thin bread from its plastic package and put it in the toaster oven. Though she considered herself a gourmet, she didn't dive into huevos rancheros or eggs Benedict first thing. Mornings had to be minimal, gentle, and predictable. She poured a glass of orange juice into what she called, in the evening, a highball glass.

Penelope's family ate breakfast together every morning. On Sundays they'd have it in her parents' room, everyone arranged on the king-size bed; if someone jangled the mattress and tea spilled on the covers, it was no big deal. Nick didn't eat breakfast with his mom, because she was usually out running before work, but they left notes for each other. Susannah was the only mother I knew who slept late (I never saw her on school days) and demanded utter silence until she was ready for conversation.

"My goodness, here's some interesting news," she said from behind the newspaper, crunching delicately into her toast. "Mrs. Cornelius Cronig finally died."

I heard the satisfaction in Susannah's first spoken words of the day. I had a good idea what it was about and couldn't let her have it so easily.

"I'm sorry to hear that." My voice dripped with concern and sorrow. "Had she been sick long?"

"Sick? No, just old. Very old." Without taking her eyes from the paper, she groped for the red marker.

"I guess you really liked her a lot."

"Hum?" She circled something on the page. "The funeral is Friday, at Lupton's."

"Poor Susannah, it must be awful when your friends start dropping off."

"Friends?" She put down the paper and I could see her eyes, no longer sleepy but focused and intent. "Neela, Mimi Cronig owns—owned—a splendid Italianate mansion on Bishop's Place. I was only there once, on the Symphony Society house and garden tour, but the interior is every bit as impressive as the exterior, I can promise you. It was—and is at this moment—filled with antiques."

"And you want them."

"Indeed I do. I intend to get them."

I heard her determination, and I knew she would succeed. "How?" I asked.

Susannah had returned to the obituaries. "Hum, Mrs. Wendell Smith died too, but she didn't have a whit of taste. There's nothing there."

I drummed my fingernails irritatingly on the tabletop.

"Stop that, Neela," she said without looking up.

"How," I repeated, "are you going to get the antiques?"

"Send flowers to her daughters."

"Do you know them?"

"Their names are listed here." She put down the paper and gazed into space. "I'll attend the funeral, of course. Then I'll follow that with a bereavement note, attaching my business card. That should do it." She pushed back from the table. "I'd better begin my day. Be a dear and put my dishes in the dishwasher, will you?"

Susannah was going up for her bath. Morning was not a time for in and out of the shower, but rather for a long soak, with bath oil, her head cushioned against the seashell-shaped plastic pillow attached by suction cups to the tub.

"Can I come up and talk to you while you take a bath?" I heard the words blurt out of me in a rush, and I didn't know where they came from. I only knew that when I was a little girl, she would sometimes let me sit on the floor and keep her company. I could only see the top of her shower cap, but I could hear her sighs and splashes, and watch her slender leg rise, with pointed toes, from the tub as she shaved it.

"Why on earth?"

"I don't know. I've got some stuff going on I'd like to talk to you about." I followed her into the front hall.

"What kind of 'stuff'?" Susannah asked hesitantly, her back to me, hand on the banister.

"I don't know." I couldn't think of a way to say it, standing in the hall, without using names: *Nick, Bertie Albrecht*. I felt too frightened to say those names to my mother. They had less power if they remained "stuff." And I couldn't give my problems a title, like *jealousy*. I couldn't allow a word like that to come to my mind, much less say it.

"Well dear, if you 'don't know,' I can't imagine how I can help you." She picked up the front of her rose-covered bathrobe, lifting the hem away from the path of her slippers. "I'll be back down in an hour or so. Perhaps we can talk then."

"Please. Now." That was all I could croak out.

"Neela. I've got to call the florist. I've got to take a bath." She turned around on the stairs to face me. "Look, we'll talk when I come down. Think about what you want to say, then organize it."

Even though Susannah made a heart-to-heart talk sound like a college application, she'd promised to give me some time, and that was something. I went into the living room and sat on a stiff Victorian couch which had only yesterday replaced a puffy, oversized sofa. For the moment the living room had a gloomy, morose look. Chairs were there to be perched on, not sat in. My favorite chair with the lion's head armrest had been sold too, so there would no longer be the cocktail hour distraction of fitting my toes around its paws.

I'd watched the band practice for another two hours. I'd tried to look interested and energetic, keeping a constant smile on my face. If Nick wanted me to do anything, help in any way, I wanted him to know I was there, ready.

The instrumentalists were totally absorbed in figuring out which songs all three might know. Bertie sat watching from the couch, too. At the other end. The spurts of music were so loud there wasn't any point trying to talk, or at least that seemed to be our excuse for not speaking. Occasionally I'd turn my smile toward her. She'd grimace back.

"Bertie, come try this out with me," Nick finally called to her. They'd just done a rendition of "Bobbie McGee" without words, sounding quite good, considering it was the first time they'd played it. Bertie lost her smile. Mine got bigger. This I had to hear. I had a feeling she was reluctant to sing because she really couldn't.

But this time she didn't protest; she went up next to Nick. He explained what he had in mind, that he'd sing lead and she'd come in on the chorus. She nodded. The band played, Nick began to sing, and the piece became music, real music held together by Nick who let the sad, funny, lonesome tune roll through him. And then Bertie moved her head close to his, so they could both use the same mike.

> "Freedom's just another word
> For nothin' left to lose . . ."

Her voice blended perfectly with his, broke when his did, their phrases beginning and ending at the same time. It seemed as though they were the song, two people who loved each other and just couldn't make it together. I even thought I heard Nick sing "Bertie McGee." It was more than I could bear.

I felt enormous tears in my eyes, tears that would

burst out of my cheeks and forehead and ears, tears that would fill up my neck and mouth and choke me if I didn't let them come. Out of pride, I tried to make myself sit there and suffer, but I was going to strangle on Bertie's success and Nick's obvious pleasure in her.

With my smile still on, I tested my trembling knees. They held me in a standing position. Very slowly, I backed over to the door and out of it. Nick was singing alone, staring ahead as though he were reading the words off the garage wall, while Bertie scrutinized his face and lip synched the words. I felt as though I were escaping a wild animal: as long as I kept my eyes on it, I would live.

Outside, my tears exploded. I ran to my car, barely able to hear my own sobs over the music coming from the garage.

> "Nothin' ain't worth nothin'
> But it's free."

I pulled out of the driveway too fast, my tires squealing as I jerked onto the road. From then on I concentrated on driving slowly, deliberately. My muscles felt frozen, and the lead weight that was my foot on the gas pedal could only be lightened by an effort of will. I checked the speedometer every few seconds. When stop signs appeared before me, my dead foot managed to switch to the brake. Traffic lights were blurs of red and green. It seemed there was only a thin line between being in control and out of control. I wondered if this was like being drunk. My sleeve stabbed at my dripping nose, my fingers pushed tears off my cheeks.

The iron gates of Arlington Place welcomed me home. The street lights were the same old-fashioned ones that once had been lit by gas, but now they gave off the warm, salmon glow of halogen. A midnight wind was blowing, and the big sycamores made shadows as they swayed. I passed Penelope's house, completely dark. I took the yellow slow-down bumps a little too fast, and the Bug groaned. I pulled up in front of number seven, our house.

As I started to get out of the car, I saw Mr. Potter lurching toward me. He wasn't singing tonight, just silently stumbling down the center of the street, coming from the direction of the boulevard. I flattened myself on the car seat. There was no rational reason to be afraid, but tonight his muteness seemed sinister.

Keeping my head under window level, I pushed down the door lock with one finger, then stretched over and locked the other door. I stopped crying, barely breathing as he passed. The only sounds were his feet scuffing on the street and an occasional, random groan. When I was sure he was past me, I peeked out at the dark, retreating figure. The street light glinted off the neck of a pint bottle stuck in his back pocket.

"Well, dear, what's on your mind?" Susannah asked. She perched on the edge of a small chair with a triangular seat. When she crossed her legs, the swish of stocking brushing against stocking cut the silence. She leaned forward, resting her chin on her fist to show interest, and her gold bracelets danced down her wrist.

"I don't really know, Susannah." I still hadn't organized my thoughts, just relived the evening.

A trio of creases formed between her eyes, and her body tensed to leave me.

"OK, OK, I do know. It's Nick."

"Nick?" She sounded so puzzled I thought she might say *Nick who?*

"I don't understand what's going on."

"Oh Baby, is that all you're worried about? I'm so relieved. From the look on your face I thought something awful had happened." She played with the rope of pearls at her chest, rolling them around her finger.

I started to say, *it has.* I started to say, *I got crazy and I ran out on Nick and he's really mad at me*, but Susannah was still talking.

"I know it must seem as though Leonard doesn't like Nick very much, but you mustn't let that bother you."

"It doesn't, Susannah. That's not . . ."

"Of course it does. It's just that they don't have much in common. Leonard adores hunting and fishing, and that evening he came to dinner . . ."

"That was last winter," I interrupted.

"Still, Leonard couldn't understand why Nick wasn't interested in going hunting with him. It wasn't your fault."

"I never thought it was. But Nick explained that he doesn't believe in killing animals."

"Well, be that as it may, I like Nick a great deal. He's an attractive, well-mannered young man, and I'm delighted you're seeing him." Susannah stood and smoothed wrinkles from her skirt lap. "Leonard will come around, don't worry."

"I know he will," I said. *As though that were the problem. As though there were going to be a Nick to come around to.*

"Look, I'm going to mention our little talk and ask him to make an effort, OK?" She pulled me toward her, pressing my forehead into the shoulder pad of her silk blouse. I smelled the diffuse, sweet scent of the perfume she dabbed under her ears. "Everything's going to be all right, I promise."

FIVE

Nick yanked open the Bug door and got in without a word.

"Hi, Nick!" I said in my most upbeat voice.

"Hi, Neela." He looked straight through the windshield. He jammed the seat belt ends together and tugged the strap tight. "What's up." It wasn't the usual question—the one that got us back with each other—but a statement that seemed to say there was no point in talking.

"Nick, don't be in a bad mood," I pleaded.

"Bad mood? You think that's what it is?"

"OK, so you're still mad." I hesitated, waiting for him to correct me.

"Let's get outta here." It was a command.

We started down Nick's driveway. Mrs. Cunningham stood up from her garden, where she'd been kneeling among tall, blue irises, waving a trowel with her muddy hand. She always seemed so friendly and welcoming. I slowed down to say hello, though I was sure she'd see through my fake smile and notice my eyes, polished by the sting of Nick's abruptness. Maybe if she did she'd say something to him later, influence him, somehow, to be nicer to me.

"Come on, keep moving," Nick ordered. "I don't want my mom getting in the middle of this."

"Nick, I was just going to be polite." But I accelerated, and fluttered my fingers as we passed her.

"Turn left," Nick ordered.

That was the direction I'd planned to turn. I didn't know if Nick had a destination in mind, but I had.

"Did you get the garage finished?" My voice once again rose up the cheerful-scale, squeezing past the dread that coated my windpipe. "How does it look?"

"The same way it did when you booked out of there the other night."

"I—"

"You—" Our words collided. We'd always been able to car-talk with incredible ease; when there was something difficult or embarrassing to say, we could do it in the car, looking straight ahead, understanding the rhythm of speech and silence. Now our words were like two fists hitting against each other, neither striking a blow where it really wanted to land, but blocking the other from hurting. I turned left again at the end of the road.

"Nick," I began once more, "I told you what happened. I was tired and I just couldn't sit there any longer. I didn't want to interrupt your session, so I just slipped out."

"Bull."

"It's the truth." My mouth was so dry that my tongue seemed to stick to my teeth, and the words came out with a funny click.

"Tell me another—I'll listen to anything." Nick carefully arranged his feet on the dashboard, sneakers flat against the glove compartment, legs doubled up almost to his chin. He locked his hands behind his neck. "Go ahead, I've got lots of time."

I concentrated on the broken yellow line that ran down the middle of the road, marveling at how straight it was, how it glowed brightly against the black asphalt in the twilight. All I had to do was keep the car to the right of that line.

"Well go ahead. Make up a better excuse."

"Nick, I don't want to fight with you. Think whatever you like."

"OK. I'll tell you what I think. You were jealous, Neela. Jealous."

The word hung huge and dripping between us. It caused blood to pound behind my ears, my palms to tingle.

"You thought I was jealous?" From far away I heard my voice flow over the word like a river roaring over a waterfall.

"I watched you a lot that night. I saw your face. I know you, Neela, and that's what it was."

The yellow center line on the road turned solid and doubled, then disappeared behind a curve. I followed it around, and there was another, sharper curve. The tires squealed.

"Hey, easy!" Nick jerked his feet down to jam on nonexistent brakes on the passenger side.

"Sorry." I prided myself on being a good driver, but I could either concentrate on Nick's words or the yellow line, not both.

"And I know what the jealousy's about, too." Nick's voice was teasing or challenging me, I couldn't tell which.

I saw Bertie as she looked three nights ago, her eyes sparkling and possessive as she came into Nick's room; her eyes earnest on me as she told me about her lifeguard job; her eyes burning on Nick as he sang the verse of "Bobbie McGee."

"Well, jealousy isn't exactly the word I would use." I tried to sound casual, praying the fear in my heart would somehow transform into confidence in my throat. "I'll admit that besides feeling tired I did have some other stuff going on, but I wouldn't call it jealousy."

"I would."

I knew I should ask, *Why?* simply, in a detached way, as though this were a debate with assigned sides to defend; but I also knew that would force him to say her name. I couldn't bear that. Just saying *Bertie* would make her real and she'd appear, all soft and fluttery, in the car. If her name was going to come up at all, I wanted to be the one who tossed it out, like the clay pigeons Leonard slung into the sky and blasted with his shotgun.

"You've been jealous of me ever since I got the Uncle Sam's job."

"Wrong." *No, right—but that was way behind me now.*

"You've been jealous ever since I started the rock group."

"Wrong again." I kept my voice flat.

"You're jealous of my time."

"Whoa, wait a minute," I said, as though I were indignant he could think such a thing. All the same, I put on the brakes. We had come to the bottom of the semicircular driveway that led up to Brentwood, our high school. "Look where we are." This was where I'd planned to take Nick when I called and said I needed to see him.

"So? We're at school, but that's not the point."

It was the point. I knew if I could get him back to school, where we'd been happy together for nine months, we could have those same feelings again. Now we wouldn't have to deal with the pressures of bells and schedules and mandatory this and that; we could have it all to ourselves, the way we wanted it. The buildings were empty and locked, the campus deserted. I circled around the old Spanish-style classroom building with its tall, arched windows and red tile roof, past the new art studio that boasted a wall of smoked glass. I drove beyond the bare parking lot and parked behind the gym, almost expecting to see the ghosts of buses and vans waiting for late afternoon games to finish. There was not a soul here.

For the first time I glanced at Nick. He still stared straight ahead, and in profile I could see a little bulge of anger that throbbed at his temple. But I had hope now, because he was on the wrong track about me. He'd said that slimy word, *jealousy*, but he hadn't said the name I linked to it as tightly as a snake coiled around a tree branch. *Bertie Albrecht*.

"Come on, Nick, let's go for a walk," I said, opening the Bug door before he had a chance to object. I stepped out of my thong sandals and left them on the grass with the same nonchalance Bertie had displayed leaving her Birkenstocks at the door of Nick's room. When I pressed my lips together, they still felt buttery from the lip gloss I'd put on half an hour before. My hair had that thick, slippery texture of fresh washing and conditioning. My gauzy Indian-print skirt swished against my legs as I walked, and my James Taylor T-shirt, which I wore for luck, came down to my hips.

The car door slammed. "Neela," Nick called, catching up to me in a few short strides, "this conversation isn't over." His fists were jammed deep in his shorts pockets; the khaki fabric stretched against the outline of his knuckles.

I heard the warning in his voice, but for me it was over. Everything would be all right, because he hadn't mentioned Bertie Albrecht. He was talking about something so removed from the core of my fear that I could handle it with ease. Jealous of the time he spent doing other things? Last week that might have been true, but today, no more. Let him spend hours, days, doing whatever he needed. As long as it wasn't with Bertie Albrecht.

Nick strode across the football field. I followed behind him, every few steps making a surge to keep up, as though I were pushing a skateboard. Stubbly grass crunched under my bare feet; dust swirled around my toes. Across the field the slim, white goalposts looked almost molten against the fading light, as though they'd been poured from the sky.

I stayed a step behind Nick until he slowed down and I saw his shoulders relax. At last, one hand slid out of his pocket. I moved beside him and put my fingers on his wrist, then skimmed them into the cup of his palm. My arms felt cold, as though I was getting a fever. He didn't squeeze my hand, but he didn't drop it either. A little further on I nuzzled my cheek against his shoulder.

Beyond the football field was a soccer-practice field, and past that, a dense grove of trees and plump hedges. This thicket formed a semicircle around the school's outdoor amphitheater—a sunken bowl with gentle, grassy sides. It was only used for graduation and the spring musical, when folding chairs would be set up along the slopes. Most of the time it was empty. Because it was too far from the school buildings for the teachers to patrol, it was a hideout for the smokers, or someone who wanted to sneak a nap, or kids like Nick and me who needed a place to be alone. And we had come here often this past spring.

I pushed him toward the amphitheater, bumping against him with my hip.

"Neela, I'm not sure this is such a hot idea," Nick said when he saw where I was headed. He hesitated, then walked faster, as though to lose me. I held so tightly to his hand that our arms snapped, like a rope towing a car. But he kept moving in the right direction. We passed through the grove, above the amphitheater, where next year Nick would have the male lead in the musical—a foregone conclusion. Nick must have been thinking about that too, because he stopped and looked down on the stage.

Then it was easy to tug him back into the grove, through the thin passageway between two bushes—a slit in the hedge you'd never notice unless you knew about it—and into the soft, damp-smelling nest of leaves. We'd always felt safe here, even when we knew there were people around. Sometimes we'd bring books, and we'd both pretend to read, while Nick lay with his head in my lap, a clipboard propped up against his thighs.

We had to crouch to get in, and then, when he started to say, "Neela," in that wary tone of his, I kissed his lips. They were wooden, pursed firmly against his teeth, his jaw set and ungiving. Humiliation spread through me, but there was no way I'd pull back. This was my chance to show how much I loved him. So I just kept my lips on his, not too softly and not too hard, just steady, until I felt him give in and kiss me back.

My arm encircled his neck, and I braced myself with my other hand, going down gently on my hip, facing him, still kissing him. Then I could put both arms around him as I lay down, drawing him on me. My mouth was open and the sweet taste of his breath, his lips, filled me with the feeling that there was nothing else in the world I wanted, only Nick.

The time was now. After months of stopping him, of saying no, I was going to do it.

I wiggled out from under him for a second, and with one hand, pulled up my T-shirt. I'd never done this before. Usually, when we made out it took a while to get to this point, and then it was his doing, his fingers I felt first against my ribs, and then at my spine, as he tentatively unhooked my bra. That had been the way I wanted it. I liked things to proceed in steps. But today I wore no bra, and when I pulled up my shirt my breasts were bare, and before we came together again, I unbuttoned his shirt so he could feel me against him. I felt my own heartbeat through his. We pressed our bodies against each other, mouths, chests, hips. His hands stroked my waist hard, as though he had to press them against me to keep from trembling. His fingers burrowed under the elastic band of my skirt. With my eyes closed, sounds were sealed off, and the world became no larger than his touch, the feeling of his hand at the edge of my panties.

Then it was gone. The pressure of him gone, the heat

gone. An icy wind had blown us apart. I didn't know what had happened. Nick was lying on his back and I was on mine.

"I don't want to do it, Neela." His voice cracked on my name.

Slowly, I reached up and pulled down my T-shirt. I didn't trust myself to speak. What did he mean, he didn't want to do it? For months it had been him pushing, saying how much he wanted me. Every time we had been alone we went farther. But it had always been me who had stopped us, for reasons I could never quite explain to myself, let alone to him. Making love was a big commitment. Maybe I was scared—not physically scared, but scared of what it meant to have sex. I knew I loved Nick so much, I was afraid to love him more.

Some of my friends kidded me about still being a virgin. Even Penelope, who'd never had a boyfriend in her life, seemed riveted whenever the subject came up. The Hereford twins had both done it and said it was no big deal except for the condom. I tried to get all the information I could from them.

Leonard and Susannah had said they wanted me to learn the truth about sex from them, not from my "peers." I began asking questions in fifth grade. The answers came in drawings of the female reproductive system. Words like "ovum" and "uterus" came easily to my parents. "Penis" was more difficult to say. When I asked more questions in seventh grade, they made the same drawings. I dropped the subject.

There had been another reason I hadn't slept with Nick yet: privacy. We usually made out on Nick's living-room couch after his mom had gone to bed, but we did it with an ear turned to the staircase. Sometimes Mrs. Cunningham came down for a bowl of yogurt if she couldn't sleep.

Susannah and Leonard had instructed me never to have Nick over when they weren't home, and for the most part I'd obeyed. But a few times when they were out we'd taken the risk and gone up to the third floor on Arlington Place. I figured if Leonard and Susannah came home early, Nick could hide out until they were asleep. It was up there, in the dusty room with plaster cracks running up the walls, that we'd almost done it. I was shaking all over when I stopped him, and he looked ready to cry. But we talked, and I told Nick I was getting ready, and he said he respected me for being sure about what I was doing. He told me I was worth the wait.

I lay on my back with the black tree leaves spinning above me. It was almost dark and very quiet. I could feel the night coolness beginning to rise through the leaves and pine needles beneath me. I shivered. One bewildered tear escaped from the corner of my eye while I waited for Nick to say something.

"It's not exactly that I don't want to, Neela." His voice seemed further away than his body. "I don't know exactly what it is. I guess I don't want to hurt you."

I sat up and looked at him. His shirt was still unbuttoned, and his chest heaved up and down as though he'd been running. Barely enough light leaked into the nest to see a small twig tangled in his curly hair and a leaf pressed into his cheek. His eyes were closed, as though what he was saying was either very painful or very boring.

92

"Don't you think that's up to me to decide?" I cried. "Don't you think after all this time and all this fooling around I know what's up?" As I heard myself say that, I felt confused. What did I mean, fooling around?

He sat up. "Look, you can't think straight right now and neither can I."

"I can think perfectly straight, Nick." I felt sobs beginning to clog my chest. "I've been thinking about it for months and so have you. Now you say you don't want to do it."

He was buttoning his shirt and tucking it in his pants. "I feel kind of stupid about the whole thing, OK? I don't know what I want at this moment."

"But it's not me, is it?"

"I don't know. Not right now." His words were muffled because his back was to me; he was crouched and already retreating through the slit in the bushes. I could have reached over and grabbed his leg, brought him back to me and kissed him and kissed him until there was no stopping. But I didn't. I was too scared to try. The leaves rustled as he pushed through.

"It's Bertie, huh?" I called. I scrambled onto my knees, groping for the opening. Her name was out, and there was no taking it back.

"No, Neela, it's got nothing to do with Bertie." His voice was far ahead of me, spread out over the soccer field into the evening.

"Well, what's it got to do with then?" I was running, my words bobbing up and down, jiggling and shaking. The grass seemed sharp as broken glass under my bare feet. I caught up to him and grabbed his arm, more to stop him than to touch him. "Answer me, Nick."

He shook off my hand. "I don't know what to say."

We were back at the Bug. He jerked open the passenger's door. Suddenly lit, the interior of the little car seemed welcoming, as though I'd turned on the light in a kitchen smelling of fresh-baked brownies. This was where I wanted to live. The car was snug and mine. The Brentwood School was dangerous; Arlington Place was dangerous. But I could open my Bug door and get in beside Nick, and everything would be cozy and OK.

"I'm sorry, Nick." It seemed I always apologized. I was good at it. If Leonard let caramel rolls burn, I apologized. If I bumped into a desk at school I apologized. If someone called and got the wrong number, I apologized.

"It's not your fault." His hand brushed the leaf from his cheek, and I watched it float to the seat with the same distress I felt each autumn when the trees declared the end of summer.

We headed down the school driveway, the car lights scooping out a silvery path. "I just want to know what's going on."

He switched on the radio. Heavy metal blared out, and Nick let his head bounce to the beat before he gave up and changed the station. We both hated heavy metal.

"It's Bertie, isn't it." I didn't have to worry about keeping her name secret anymore. I could say it whenever I wanted. I could scream it, or whisper it, or make it sarcastic. I could make *Bertie* sound stupid.

"Neela, let it rest. Bertie's my next-door neighbor. We grew up together. Give me a break." He fiddled with the radio dial and found the oldies station.

Neither of us said anything the whole drive to Nick's house. The music all seemed to have meaning. Aretha

Franklin asked for "Respect." "I Heard It Through the Grapevine." But when James Taylor sang "Fire and Rain," I quietly lost it. "I always thought that I'd see you again." I don't know if Nick could hear me snuffling up the tears.

The Cunninghams' house was dark even though it was still early. "Guess Mom's gone to the movies or something," Nick said. He opened the Bug door, and when the light went on it was like we were the movie, a big, bright screen that everyone could stare at.

I waited for him to invite me in.

"I feel like a jerk for having it end up like this," he said. He was picking at his cuticle so he wouldn't have to look at me.

My heart hammered *end up, end up, end up. End up* for the evening or for good? I didn't want to know.

"Can I call you sometime?" I asked at last, hoping it somehow sounded casual.

"Whatever."

"Well, can I call you tomorrow?"

I planned to flee by the quickest possible route. Once I read about convicts escaping from prison by helicopter, and now I was desperate to be plucked up from this anguish and zoomed into the sky. Instead, I found myself driving halfway down Nick's driveway, turning off the headlights, and putting on the emergency brake. With the engine off, I could hear the early summer night around me—peepers or crickets or something—sounds that were foreign to Arlington Place, where night noises were traffic from the boulevard, Mr. Potter's drunken bellowing, the dogs barking.

I twisted around, peering between the high seat backs

of the Bug, and checked out Nick's house. The sharp blaze of an overhead light had gone on in his bedroom. His shades were up, and a few seconds later I saw him cross the window with the blurry impression of a cat streaking in front of a headlight. I knew every detail of that room. He was heading toward the bed. It was only eight-thirty; there was no way Nick was going to sleep now. But the phone was next to his bed, and when I didn't see him come back across the window, I knew what he was doing. He was talking to Bertie Albrecht.

It wouldn't do any good to sneak back under his window; I'd never hear his voice from that far away. I knew how he stretched out on the bed when he talked, the phone tucked between his chin and shoulder so he could mess with his guitar at the same time. He didn't play it, but let a few chords slide from under his fingers, as though he were on stage talking through an introduction, backing it with warm-up. Sometimes he'd give me little phone tests, trying to get me to identify chords, though he knew I couldn't tell the difference between an A minor and a B7 if I were in front of a firing squad. Now I pictured him cooing to Bertie, caressing the guitar. I wondered if you could harmonize over the phone.

Suddenly he moved across the window again, fast, and the light went out. Blood rushed to my head. I knew where he was going. He was in the hall, now trotting down the stairs. Quickly, I turned on the ignition. If I could be out of the driveway by the time he hit the front door, I'd be safe. I'd be just another car passing the house on the road. *He's on his way to Bertie's, and I can't let him catch me spying.*

Panic transported me home so quickly it seemed as though the helicopter had indeed yanked me from the prison yard. I passed Penelope's house and shivered with loneliness. Not even Mr. Potter was on the street. I looked up at our house as I parked and saw lights in the windows like a checkerboard: Aunt Amelia's third-floor apartment glowed through the curtains; Leonard and Susannah's bedside light was on in their room; the Tiffany lamps were on in the living room. Trying to be as quiet as possible, I let myself in the front door.

Susannah sat on the Victorian couch—which I was sure would never sell, it was so chunky and dark and hideous. She'd folded the newspaper to cushion the crossword puzzle, and she tapped her cheek with a pencil. "Neela, what an unusual hour for you to get home."

"I've been home by nine before," I said defensively.

"True, but I remember when I was your age and went out with my young man—" she interrupted herself to reach for her half-filled drink on the coffee table—"I made the night last as long as possible." She took a sip from the glass, looking up at me quizzically.

"Where's Leonard?"

"Asleep, poor dear."

"I'm hungry," I said, turning toward the kitchen.

"You'll get fat eating before bed," she called. Her voice was thick and singsongy.

She's right, I thought, as I gazed in the refrigerator— four kinds of smelly cheese, a package of carrots, black olives, green olives, leftover eggplant Parmesan. I already felt as wretched and ugly as the Victorian couch, so I took a spoon and dug away at a rock-hard container of ice cream from the freezer. When I'd wrenched out a few bites, I rinsed the spoon and put it in the dishwasher. Leonard demanded that the kitchen be spotless.

I had to get upstairs. I had to be alone, to figure out

what had happened tonight. I wanted to sneak up the back steps and avoid Susannah completely, but I knew if I did, in half an hour she'd barge into my room. I'd handle it in the straightforward, mature way. "I'm going up now, good night," I called as I passed through the hall.

"Wait a minute."

I stopped, one foot on the stairs.

"Come back in here." Her voice was even thicker, as though it was collecting sludge.

I pivoted and dragged myself to the living room. Through the window I at last heard Mr. Potter, snorting and roaring on his way home. Susannah stared down at her crossword puzzle, erasing a word square by square.

"Sit down, dear," she said without looking up. "Leonard's gone to bed. Let's share some quality time."

"Susannah, please."

"No no, come on, we haven't talked in ages." She nodded at the uncomfortable triangular chair, while still studying her crossword puzzle.

I sat, and sighed a huge, meaningful sigh. "What do you want to talk about?" No way she was going to find out about Nick.

"What's a six letter word for protoplasm?"

My heart was broken, and she had questions about biology. "I have no idea."

"Of course you do. Everyone your age knows. You go to school."

"Susannah, I'm going to bed."

"Don't go yet. Let's talk. The fifth letter is *b*. It's so hard to remember details when you've been out of school so long."

I looked at her glass, where the amber liquid had sunk

down to the last inch. "It's hard to remember details when you're drinking scotch." I didn't know where I got the nerve to say that.

There was an ominous silence in the room. She raised her eyes, leading with her chin and nose, until her face was pointed up and she could look down on me from a superior angle. "Is that," her words were precise now, "supposed to mean something?"

I didn't know what it was supposed to mean. I felt so bewildered and exhausted. When I tried to collect my feelings about scotch and Susannah, all I could think of was Nick striding across the field, Nick pushing away from me. I had my own problems. I didn't want to think about what Susannah's nightly drinks meant. I felt near tears again, and I didn't know who they were for.

"Hum?"

That was supposed to mean, *Come on now, say something. Answer me.* But I couldn't even remember the question. I stood up. "I can't deal with this right now."

"Well, you'd better be more careful with those snippy little comments, miss." Her mouth was working to pronounce the syllables carefully, but the sludge coated each word.

I ran from the room and up the red-carpeted stairs. I stopped on the landing to catch my breath and looked around at the prints and paintings of yachts racing, billowing sails in great winds, boats moored at rest in harbors, the *Titanic* ready to hit the iceberg. Suddenly I thought of Susannah's scotch like an oil spill, contaminating and dirtying everything it touched, killing the wildlife. I turned and leaned over the banister.

"*Amoeba*," I shouted. "Protoplasm. Fifth letter *b*."

SIX

Dear Penelope,

Where are you? Oh yeah, I remember—at camp, you traitor. You're having a fabulous time with a zillion friends and your precious horse. But you know where you should be—right here. I keep passing your house and waiting for the light in your room to go on. You and I should be in there talking. You'd tell me what to do, and you'd tell me the truth, I know you would. I've lost Nick and I don't know what's going on. I'm so miserable and confused right now, and so . . .

I put down my pen and tried to imagine Penelope getting a letter like the one that was now babbling out of me. I couldn't remember ever being so lonely. I couldn't remember ever needing a friend so much. But this wasn't the kind of letter friends looked forward to opening. I tore it up.

Hey Penelope,

How's it going, girl? I thought you'd want to know that even though I really miss you, things are still alive and pretty much the same on Arlington Place. Your house looks weird at night without a light on in your room, but that's about the biggest change in the block. Mr. Potter still is polluted every night, so the world goes on. I guess the only change in my life is that Nick and I aren't seeing as much of each other as we used to.

I couldn't finish that letter either. It was too dishonest. If I couldn't write her the truth, then I wouldn't write anything. Penelope would be back in two weeks—approximately 336 hours from now. What good would it do to write a letter, anyway? She wasn't going to fly home to hold my hand.

I put my head down on my desk, cupping my forehead in my hands, my palms pressed into my eyes. The little explosions of red and yellow lights I saw in the blackness, like fireworks in my brain, diverted me for a few seconds from my misery. But only a few. It had been four days since Nick shattered my life. I saw him in deep twilight, marching back across the soccer field, a leaf still pressed in his cheek. *It's not exactly that I don't want to, Neela.* Well then, what did he want?

Ever since that terrible night I'd been exhausted. I'd slept hard every night and awakened late, unable to remember any dreams. Still, I'd feel sleepy again a few hours after I got up and doze off baby-sitting Susannah's telephone. I tried to distract myself by reading, but I kept feeling a buzz behind my eyelids, and soon I had to close them. Whenever I was awake Nick was there, growing larger and more important in my head.

I tried to figure out why I loved him so much. One thing I knew: When I was with him I felt safe. Our intimacy was like a crackling fire that heated every part of me, yet warned others away with its flames. Susannah couldn't get to me, Leonard couldn't reach me.

I opened the desk drawer and took his picture from under the sketch pads. There he was, mellow-eyed, his arm still making room for me to snuggle against him. He still looked like the person who had loved me, who had wanted to kiss and touch me. I stared at that photograph. I brought my eyes close to it. I rubbed it with my thumb, as though to sand off a layer of deceit. All I could see in it was his gentleness and kindness. I couldn't see the person who was angry at me, who ignored me sometimes, who maybe flirted with other girls. I knew those parts of him were there, but they weren't in my picture.

I ran up the stairs—or they moved under me independently, like a speeded-up escalator. I was deposited on the landing of a strange building—no, it was our house. I knocked on Aunt Amelia's door, unaware I'd done it until I heard my knuckles echo back at me. I pressed my ear to the door panel, where the wood was thinnest. Silence. Then a swishing, which would be feet in house slippers shuffling across the sitting room, and then a few long moments of silence again. She must be deciding whether or not to answer. She must be standing with her hand on the knob.

"Yes?" The door creaked open. I looked up into her stern, tight face.

"Sorry to bother you," I said, backing up.

"Well?"

"Well, hi," I began, with a nervous laugh.

"What may I do for you?" The door opening narrowed.

"I've got . . ." I began, but my lungs didn't have breath to finish the sentence.

"You look terrible," she interrupted.

"I've got a problem." My voice broke.

"We all have problems." It was a short, matter-of-fact statement, but her tone became softer. I was supposed to say something in the pause that followed, but I couldn't. "And you think I could help?" she finally added.

"I hope so," I whispered, my voice barely recovered.

"In that case I probably can't do it in the hall. You'd better come inside."

The air-conditioned room smelled metal-cold and made my skin pucker. I sank into the soft leather couch, which seemed to grab and pull me down, though I'd only meant to perch on the edge. Aunt Amelia lowered herself stiffly into the rocking chair.

"All right. Get yourself together and tell me what the problem is."

"It's not that easy."

"It never is. Go ahead. Start." The rocking chair groaned back and settled into rhythmic thumps.

I sorted through possible beginnings. They all started with the word *Nick*. Aunt Amelia kept rocking.

"Let me take a stab at it," she said.

Did I have Nick all over my face? Was he oozing out my pores?

The chair stopped, and Aunt Amelia leaned forward, veiny hands pressed on her knees. "You're bored."

Bored. That was supposed to be Nick's problem, not mine. He was the one who'd been worried about that. I'd been planning to have him, and he was never boring.

"So, why don't you get a job?"

"A job?" The word tripped me up for a second. "Well, I promised Susannah I'd help her this summer. Anyway, it's too late to get a job. But I thought maybe . . ."

"It's never too late to do anything we set out to do."

"Right. But I've had this idea."

"Ideas are one thing. Actions are another."

"Aunt Amelia."

"Yes?"

"Can I borrow a camera from you?"

Her face dissolved, in slow motion, from interest in my problem into horror. Then she swallowed that feeling—actually swallowed it, with movement in her throat that caused a squeak—and recomposed herself. "Why would you want to borrow a camera?"

I shrugged. I had to play this low-key. "I don't know. I thought it would be neat to learn to take pictures. Good ones, that show everything clearly."

She settled her elbows onto the armrests and tilted her head back. She closed her eyes. "Don't your parents have a camera?"

"Susannah has a Polaroid for taking pictures of antiques, but that's not what I need—I mean—what I want. Her pictures look too fuzzy."

"What about your friends? It seems that every third child alive has an expensive camera now." She continued rocking with closed eyes.

"My friends are away on vacation. But anyway, they all have point-and-shoot cameras. I want something that will take pictures without the flash going off all the time."

"You do? Why?"

This was a critical moment. I had to come up with

a reason that sounded valid—maybe even artistic. "I like the way people and scenery look in natural light." I remembered the tissue-covered photograph I'd glimpsed in the box in her bedroom. "What I really like are black-and-white pictures."

Her eyes were open, and fixed on my face. "Really." There was total disbelief in that word.

"Really," I repeated, trying not to sound sarcastic, but terribly sincere.

"If you want to take black-and-white photographs, you certainly are part of a dwindling minority."

I shrugged. "It's what the photo staff of *The Guardian*—our school paper—uses."

She folded her arms. She studied me. "Very interesting. And what, may I ask, do you know about making photographs?"

"Nothing, Aunt Amelia. But I thought maybe . . ."

"You did, did you?"

"Maybe . . ."

"Maybe you could borrow a camera and I could teach you to use it."

I nodded.

"Because you're bored, and this would make the summer go by."

I nodded again. She hadn't seen Nick. He wasn't visible to everyone, only me.

"I'm afraid you've come to the wrong person." She'd eased stiff bones into the rocker, but now she jumped out of it as though her body had no age. "Impossible." She paced over to the window and back, while I sat looking up at her from the couch.

"Please," I begged.

"I don't want to get involved in photography again. There are too many memories."

"You don't have to get involved, Aunt Amelia, just show me a couple of things," I pleaded.

"You don't understand a thing, child. You have no idea what heartache it is to even think about my work. I'm sorry now I built a darkroom here. When Oliver died, that part of my life was over. It still is."

"Why did you buy all that darkroom stuff the other day, then?"

She stopped pacing, and seemed to grow taller as she stared down at me. "Because," she began and fell silent. "Because the pain of memory lifted for a short time, and I fell back in my old habits. A mistake, I can promise you. I've paid for it dearly in gray days and sleepless nights. I can't go through that kind of thing again."

I felt all my newly found energy and enthusiasm drain from me. Seventeen years of experience with Susannah and Leonard told me when an answer was no. This was one of those times. I didn't know how to argue her out of her position.

"Never mind, Aunt Amelia," I said as I pushed my way up from the soft couch. The leather cushion clung briefly to the back of my legs, then released me.

"Oh don't say that. I can't bear the expression 'never mind.' Of course you mind. I mind too, which you may find hard to believe. But there's just nothing we can do about it right now."

"Yoo-hoo!" Susannah called on two melodious notes, and then sang out another three, "I'm ho-ome."

Released. I ran from my room down the hall stairs, bouncing lightly off the royal-red carpet. I couldn't wait to get out of the house.

"Any messages, lambie?" Susannah must have had a profitable afternoon to be so cheery.

I consulted the steno pad next to the back hall phone. "Mrs. Dexter called about some silver tray. Said she wanted it for her niece's birthday or wedding or something."

"Just which silver tray did she want, Neela?" We were back to normal. Her voice had sharpened up and, of course, I had no idea which silver tray. I also had to tell her that Mrs. Allyn was returning a desk because she said it had a huge scratch that hadn't been there when she chose it.

Susannah's arms went stiff at the elbows, and her long, crimson fingernails dug into her palms. Her lower jaw clamped forward. Her eyes glittered, then narrowed. "That dreadful, dreadful woman," she hissed. "After all I've done for her. After all the hours I've wasted. To accuse me of scratching a desk." She whirled around and grabbed the phone.

I fled.

My little orange Bug waited for me outside the front door, as the pumpkin had waited for Cinderella. The trouble was, I had nowhere to go. But when I got in and started the motor, the Bug headed through the gates of Arlington Place as though it were not being steered by me but pulled by mice. It made all turns with precision, almost on its own. And soon it became clear, we were headed to Nick's house.

• • •

"Neela!" Mrs. Cunningham called from her flower bed as I drove up the drive. I wanted to slam the Bug in reverse, but it was too late. I stopped. She walked toward my open window.

A battered straw hat shaded her face from the late afternoon sun, but that was the only evidence of an old-fashioned gardener. She weeded in cut-off jeans and a fluorescent-pink halter. Her feet were bare.

"Hi, Mrs. Cunningham. I thought you were at work." That second part slipped out too fast.

"Hi there, Neela." She stuck her hand in the window and rubbed my cheek with her knuckles. "I should be at work, but I played hooky today. Couldn't let these weeds take over. What's new?"

What's new? Hadn't she heard? Didn't she know that even though this week I'd talked to her three times on the phone, and I was sure she'd passed the message on to Nick, he had never called back? Didn't she know that we didn't seem to be going out together anymore?

"Not much," I lied.

"Come on in, have some iced tea. Nick will be home soon. It's one of his early days."

"No thanks, I'm fine Mrs. Cunningham."

"I'm sure you are, but what a scorcher it's been today. I need a break." She had taken off her hat and was rumpling her flattened-down hair. "Come keep me company." She started walking toward the house.

If Nick didn't want to talk to me on the phone, how was he going to feel about finding me in his kitchen? I didn't know why I'd even come to his house. I didn't know if I thought I'd find Nick and his mom home, or if I really thought they'd both be out. But I did know I liked Mrs. Cunningham, and that she and Nick were very tight. I thought they had a special relationship because his father had split, and Nick had to take his place. Once I made the mistake of expounding my theory to Nick. "That's Psych 101 bullshit," he'd said. "Mom and I are friends because she's a good mom."

The Cunninghams' kitchen was like an extension of the garden. Plants were jammed on the windowsills and trailed down the walls. Bunches of fresh herbs had been hung to dry from the exposed rafters. In one corner stood a pile of baskets, ready to harvest the garden or sit on the counter full of fresh fruit.

Mrs. Cunningham tossed her straw hat onto the wooden table and opened the refrigerator door. She took out the iced-tea pitcher, which left a big space on the top shelf. As I blotted beads of sweat off my forehead, I could imagine crawling onto the shelf, rolling myself into a ball—like a cantaloupe—and living in the refrigerator. I'd be cool and hidden there. Nick could walk into this kitchen at any moment.

"Nick said you're working for your mother's business this summer," she said as she plopped ice cubes into two glasses.

"Kind of."

"How's it going?"

Now there was a question. Wouldn't she be surprised by the real answer: *Terrible. Horrible. Lonely.* "It hasn't been the greatest," I said, venturing a shade of the truth.

"Oh? I'm sorry, Neela." She held up her glass to clink against mine, as though we were toasting something. "Here's to things picking up. And they will, you know."

I took a long drink of my tea to drown my confusion.

She didn't seem to know a thing about this mess. She didn't realize that it was her son causing my unhappiness—her son and Bertie Albrecht. Or maybe she did know about it. Maybe she said things would "pick up" because she assumed Bertie was only a slight detour in my relationship with Nick. Maybe she thought he'd be back to me soon.

Hope made me dare a look into her eyes; I had to find out where I stood. Her eyes were as welcoming and soft as Nick's were in the photograph. I wanted to tell her everything.

"Things have changed, Mrs. Cunningham."

"I'm afraid that's both the most difficult and exciting thing about life—change. I've been through a bit of that myself." She looked at me with a direct, ironic half-smile, and I thought of Nick's father, roaring off on his motorcycle. "But I think I know what you mean."

"Has Nick talked to you? About me?"

"Not much. What goes on between the two of you is between the two of you. But I can see something's different."

"It is," I said, tracing the sweat circles the glass left on the kitchen table.

"Forgot lemons for the tea," she said, opening the fridge again. Was she trying to change the subject?

I watched her cut a lemon wedge, slicing cleanly through the rind and pulp. "Mrs. Cunningham, maybe you could do something. Talk to Nick for me. Please."

"Neela, whatever the problem, I'd never get involved in your business or in Nick's business that way." She squeezed lemon juice in our glasses, still smiling a little.

"But Nick trusts you. I've never heard him talk about

you the way other kids talk about their parents." My voice was spiraling up in desperation. "You could tell him how important he is to me."

Mrs. Cunningham locked her hands together and rested her chin on them. Her eyes were steady. "If he trusts me it's because I trust him to make personal decisions. And I have complete faith in you. If there's anything you need to say to Nick, you'll be able to do it."

"I can't," I cried. "I'm all twisted up."

"Maybe you are right now. But you'll straighten out. You'll do what's best for you, I know it."

I felt tears pushing inside me, waiting to burst from my eyes, my ears, my fingers. I couldn't bear it that she had such faith in me. I didn't know why she thought I'd do the best for myself, when I felt my heart ripped out and the pain of it consuming me.

I heard the sound of car tires on the gravel drive. I went rigid. There was no escape: the Bug was in the driveway. I couldn't slip out the kitchen door. Never, never again would I be caught in this humiliating position. The car door slammed.

"That's not Nick," Mrs. Cunningham said. "He took his bicycle to work."

I was so relieved I giggled. Of course it wasn't Nick; he didn't have a car.

"Yo, Mrs. C.," called a voice from the hall.

"In the kitchen, Bob," she answered. In a second the door frame was filled by the lanky frame of Wolf Man, the drummer.

I thought I saw his expression change when he saw me, just a tremor, before he said, "Neela! What's up?"

"Not much," I said, glancing at Mrs. Cunningham.

111

She looked pleasant and composed, not at all as though we'd just been having an intense conversation.

Wolf Man engulfed a kitchen chair, swinging the back of it through his legs and straddling the seat as though he were on a motorcycle. He hunched over and with two fingers of each hand began thumping on the table edge. He pounded to a crescendo, and with a final whack to his leg and chest, looked up at us. "Where's Nick?"

"Uncle Sam's," Mrs. Cunningham said. "He'll be home any minute."

That was my cue. It wasn't too late. I could still get out. "I've got to get home myself. It's almost dinner time," I said. Dinner would not really be for hours, since Leonard was cooking tonight. "Thanks for the iced tea, Mrs. Cunningham."

"Iced tea? You been holding out on me, Mrs. C.?" Wolf Man asked, as he hit an invisible cymbal above his head.

Mrs. Cunningham seemed to understand that I wanted to get out of there, fast. She didn't try to hold me up with conversation. "'Bye, Neela. I always love seeing you." And the fact that I could tell she meant it almost brought back tears.

"Hey, aren't you waiting for Nick?" Wolf Man asked, suddenly paying attention.

I shook my head. I left. As I opened the Bug door, Wolf Man's head appeared at the screened window, calling to me. "But we're having a practice tonight. Don't you want to watch?"

I threaded my way down Arlington Place, around a group of kids playing baseball in the street, over the yellow speed bumps, past the Steiner kids on their skateboards. I glanced at Penelope's window. Both Leonard's car and Susannah's were parked in front of our house. A sprinkler arched lazily over our patchy lawn and settled at one end of its sweep for a long soak of the front steps; on its way back, I started into the house.

The time I spent socializing Liver, Bacon, and Onions seemed to be working. I could hear the frantic scratch of toenails on the wooden floor as they raced to the door, but the dogs recognized me, and there was no barking. They stood sentry at the screen door, with throaty little yelps of anticipation. They even wagged their tails— Liver's a long plume, Onions' sleek and tapered, Bacon's a stump that seemed to wag him.

"Where have you been?" Susannah demanded. She peered over her half-frame reading glasses. A yellow legal pad lay in her lap. The lacquered tray with the martini pitcher was on the coffee table.

"I had an errand," I replied breezily, repeating the very phrase Susannah used so often.

"Don't be so glib," Leonard said, as he came into the room and scratched my head on the way to his chair. "Have you locked the screen door so the dogs can't get out? Yes? Then go get yourself a glass of something and join us."

In the kitchen I took a plastic tumbler with a fishing fly and hook sandwiched between thermal layers. I poured a glass of orange juice. Then I was drawn to the counter, which glittered with bottles. They'd never before looked so alluring. I examined each label. Gin. Vodka. Two kinds of scotch. Bourbon. I picked up the dusty bottles in the back row, with foreign names—

cognac, crème de menthe, even something called Afri-coco.

Because almost all the kids from Brentwood went to college, we were supposed to be the cream of the crop. We were supposed to be dedicated to excellence in our pursuit of academics, athletics, and moral values. We weren't the kind of kids who were dopers or got wasted every night. Or we weren't supposed to be.

In truth, the first time I ever saw any pot was when a sophomore girl tried to sell me a joint in the lunch line. I was in seventh grade. I knew Mary Lou Atkins kept a pint bottle in her hall locker and took a swig every time she got out a book. The teachers had no idea. And lots of kids bragged about getting wasted on the weekends.

I'd never been tempted. Kids would sneak bottles into school parties, but it just didn't interest me. I'd always been able to have fun without it. Penelope didn't drink, and neither did my other good friends—the Hereford twins, Susan Margolis, Janice Oldenbach. Nick didn't drink. He said last summer he smoked some because it was the cool thing to do, but he really didn't like the way it slowed his mind down. And it didn't help his guitar work, either.

I couldn't stand the idea of another night at home alone with Susannah and Leonard. I didn't want to watch TV or read in my room. I couldn't think of anyone to hang out with. I just wanted the evening to pass as quickly as it possibly could. I wanted out.

I knew what gin tasted like and it was repulsive. I unscrewed the top of the bourbon bottle, took a sniff, and reeled back. No way. Vodka. That's what Mary Lou kept in her locker. She said it was the one drink that wouldn't show up on your breath.

Several times Leonard had said to me, "If you're going to drink, learn to do it at home. Tell me when you want a drink, and I'll teach you to mix it properly." But I knew if I walked in there and said, "OK, Leonard, this is it. I want a drink," the reaction would be off the wall. He'd fling around phrases like "age-appropriate activities." But I also knew I could help myself to anything I wanted on the counter without it being missed. No one kept track of how quickly the level fell in the gin bottle. There were new bottles to take the place of empties on the top shelf of the pantry closet. Vodka was for guests. A drink or two would never be noticed. If I took it in the living room, sat down normal as could be, Susannah and Leonard would have no idea what was going on.

I drank half my glass of orange juice and filled the remainder with vodka. The time I'd drained the martini pitcher, my throat had been on fire, but the first sip of this told me it wasn't that bad. Instead of fire there was just a warmth that gently toasted my cheeks and forehead. This was more like it.

"Neela!" Leonard called from the living room.

"Coming," I yelled back, and poured another slug into my glass.

I was all smiles as I sat down. Who cared that I no longer had my lion's paws chair to curl my toes over? Who cared that Susannah was writing some sort of list, while Leonard read *Field and Stream*? I became absorbed in studying the color of my socks, one of which had gotten bleached with the whites in the laundry. I tried to figure out how different the hues were. Casually, I sipped my drink.

"Well," Leonard said finishing his article and setting down the magazine. "Very interesting."

"Riveting, I'm sure," I said, and gave him a dazzling smile. I took another swallow of orange juice.

"Bertha Babcock is on," Susannah began to intone. "Gertrude Allyn is absolutely off. Both Mrs. Cornelius Cronig's daughters are on."

"That would be the late, poor, dead Mimi Cronig?" I asked, with another gorgeous smile.

"Enough, Neela. What are you working on, dear?" Leonard asked.

"The list for my tea," Susannah said. Without looking up, her hand wandered over to her martini glass. "Roberta Metz is on. What about Martha Radford? She doesn't buy antiques, but she is a good neighbor." She was asking me if Penelope's mother should be invited.

I drained my glass. "Give me a second to think about it," I said. Leonard had returned to reading his magazine. I went out to the pantry to make another drink. My arm felt disconnected from my body as I poured vodka in the glass. I spilled some orange juice and admired the way it spread out on the counter.

On the way back to the living room I stumbled against Bacon, snoozing half under a dining-room table. He gave a little howl.

"Sorry, Bacon old buddy," I murmured, and carefully put my drink down. I suddenly found myself on my knees, my nose next to his cold one. "Good old Bacon," I crooned over and over.

"Why are you addressing that dog as Bacon?" Leonard called from the living room. "Heel, King," he ordered, snapping his fingers. Bacon left.

The dining-room floor seemed like a nice place to stay. The rug was scratchy on my cheek, but I could see why Bacon liked to lie under the table. I'd lie further under it, all the way, where no one could find me.

"Neela," Susannah called sharply. I hopped up as quickly as Bacon, and banged my head. Hard. "Yow!" I cried.

"What's going on in there?"

"Hit my head."

"Poor dear, how did you manage that?"

I stood up and felt dizzy. But I knew it wasn't the bump on the head. It was a sick, spiraling feeling that came up through my stomach. I grabbed my drink, and tottered into the living room.

"What on earth is wrong with you?"

"Banged my head."

"I do think Martha Radford really would enjoy it, don't you?"

"I'm going to have a lump there." I rubbed my scalp.

"Though she may be out of town then," Susannah mused.

"Bacon made me."

"You're not making a whit of sense."

I had to get out. Like Susannah late at night, I would pronounce my words with great care. "Excuse me, please. I'm going upstairs. I don't want supper tonight. It's too hot." I spit out the word *hot*, my final effort.

"As you will," Leonard sighed. "But you're missing what promises to be an excellent veal marsala."

I held onto my drink, squeezing it as though it were the head of a cane that would get me upstairs. Veal marsala. I could see the thin pieces of gray meat packaged in plastic. I could smell the sizzling wine as Leonard poured it over the meat. My stomach tightened.

117

Upstairs, I rushed into the bathroom and poured the drink down the drain. I splashed my face with cold water. The room kept tilting. I didn't think I was going to be sick, but I couldn't be sure, so I stayed there quite a while, just sitting on the toilet seat. I hated the way I felt. This wasn't what I'd meant when I opened the vodka bottle.

At last my stomach was steady enough to let me go into my own room. With huge relief I saw my wonderful canopy bed and was ready to fling myself on it. But there was already something there.

A camera.

There was a note next to the camera, written in pencil on a square of brown, grocery-bag paper. The hand-writing would have been difficult to decipher even if I hadn't still had the whirlies. I had to concentrate on each word separately in order to read.

Come see me at 8:30 tomorrow and we'll begin work. I'm not promising anything, but perhaps I can help after all.

Aunt A.

SEVEN

I slept in my clothes. I woke up at dawn, my parched mouth filled by a cotton tongue. My head felt like a giant jack-o'-lantern, hollowed out, leaving only an aching hole. Through burning slits called eyes, I saw Aunt Amelia's camera on my chair. I reread the note: *8:30*, she said.

Two hours later the alarm went off. My limbs still ached, my head throbbed. I looked at myself in the bathroom mirror, skin slightly gray, with livid pink pillow creases etched in my cheek like knife scars. When I'd been a kid, and boys were just an idea, I'd practiced kissing the mirror. I loved the way my face looked coming toward itself, before my steamy breath smudged the spot where my lips would meet the glass. Today I felt as young and dumb as I had been then. Staring at my glazed face in the mirror, I couldn't imagine anyone wanting to kiss me.

A long shower helped. Even Leonard's bog-brew coffee helped.

At eight-thirty precisely, with Aunt Amelia's camera clutched in my hand, I knocked on her door.

"Oh dear," she gasped, stepping back. She evaluated me from underneath her brown, feather-penciled eyebrows. "You looked dreadful yesterday, but today you look even worse."

She didn't look so hot herself. Little gray hammocks of skin hung under her eyes. Her lipstick melted into spiny puckers around the edge of her lips. If she were to smile and show her teeth, I'd probably see that her incisors had turned to fangs overnight. It seemed a health hazard to commit so much as an hour of my day to this woman, who—even without fangs—could rip and gnaw me with her words.

"Do come in," she said impatiently.

I halted in the doorway, pinned between fear of Aunt Amelia and my need to learn about this camera. I also had an uneasy feeling that she could see the truth. I'd told her I wasn't much of a drinker, but I'd been totally trashed last night. She said I looked terrible: I was afraid she knew why. She also might know the real reason I wanted to take pictures.

"Come in, come in." She gestured me in the door with a loose-wristed hand flap, like a cop moving a line of traffic. "It doesn't matter how you look, as long as you're alert enough to work. Step inside, now. We've got a lot to do."

I moved mechanically into the room. The door closed.

"There's one thing I want to make clear before we start," she said, gripping her hands. "We must be candid with each other, or this will never work. I'm not sure quite why I've agreed to take you on." She looked straight at me with that arched gaze of hers. "I don't want to make photographs again, but my common sense tells me that *you* taking pictures isn't the same as *me* doing it. So I've decided to try and teach you what I can. But if it gets too hard for either of us, we both must be able to get out with no hurt feelings." Her eyebrows flexed up. "Agreed?"

All I could feel was relief. The possibility that I could get out without a failing grade was an incredible comfort. Because, no matter what she said, it seemed more likely that I'd be the one who'd bolt.

I nodded in agreement, still mute.

"Let's get started. What's that thing you're holding in your hand?"

"A camera?"

"A thirty-five millimeter camera. A camera that's been to Africa and Asia, Europe, and most every one of our states. It's twenty-five years old now, and good as the day it was bought."

The camera she'd lent me looked old-fashioned in some ways, yet extremely high-tech in others. It was black metal and dull stainless steel, and consisted, I learned, of two parts: the body and the lens. The body had gizmos on the top, all of which Aunt Amelia explained—the film advance, film counter, film winder, and shutter.

"Now that you know the proper names for the camera parts, you need no longer say gizmos," she said.

The lens looked straightforward enough, except for the numbers and arrows engraved on the side. It was a zoom lens, and Aunt Amelia showed me how it could be adjusted from wide angle to telephoto. Then she began to use terms like "shutter speed" and "f-stop" and "depth of field," and talk about the relationships among them.

I begged her not to get too technical.

"There's a good deal to learn, all right. It takes time and practice to let the vocabulary sink in, but you'll get it. You're a smart girl. Meanwhile, let's just look at the light meter."

On the camera back was the viewfinder. When I put my eye to it, I saw a gray, rectangular line that defined the edges of my pictures, and on the side, a needle that could be moved—the light meter. Aunt Amelia told me how it worked, that it measured whether enough light would get to the film to make a proper exposure.

Then she pulled a roll of film out of her desk drawer. She showed me how to load the camera, threading one end of the film through the winder, and not shutting the camera back until I'd made sure the film was caught.

Once again we went over how to use the light meter, and this time it didn't seem so hard: If I kept the shutter speed consistent, and adjusted the f-stops until the exposure needle was centered, and focused the lens, I could take a picture.

"That's all there is to it," she said, handing the camera to me. "For now."

"Oh, that's all?" I repeated with a trace of sarcasm. My head was jammed with information. Concepts that numbers people like Nick could learn easily sent a math-dodo and technology-dumb-dumb like me into a sweat.

"As a matter of fact, no, that is *not* all. There's still another essential thing." Aunt Amelia clamped her thumb and fingers together into a circle, put it to her left eye, and squeezed the other eye shut. She turned straight to me, her eye blazing through the imaginary lens. "You. You're the most important part of any picture. It's what

122

you choose to see, and when you decide to squeeze the shutter that counts." She scanned the room, now and then stopping as though she'd found her picture, and I could feel the intensity of her concentration.

I stood there, the camera awkwardly in my hand.

"Go on, now. You'll never take a photograph just holding it," she said, still looking through her hand-lens.

"What should I do?"

She pointed her make-believe camera to the wall clock. Almost three hours had passed. "There are thirty-six exposures on your roll of film. Use them all. Make thirty-six pictures. Don't worry about how they're going to come out, just think about what you want and take them. And then we'll meet back here at six o'clock." She dropped her circled fingers and opened her other eye. "If I remember correctly that's the cocktail hour, isn't it?"

Susannah was out; the house was empty. I stood in the center of my room, turning around slowly, collecting in my head all the things that meant Nick. I was going to photograph every one of them. I was going to make every-thing connected with him permanent, make him mine forever.

I took the picture of Nick from my desk. I loved that picture—and I hated it because Bertie Albrecht had taken it. It was all I had for now. I propped it against my silver brush on the dressing table. I always thought about Nick when I brushed my hair, in the morning, before a date, again before I went to bed. My first photograph would be a picture of his picture.

I hoisted the camera up. It felt heavy, as though it had gained weight since leaving Aunt Amelia's. I clamped my eye to the viewfinder and squeezed the other eye shut.

Blackout. I couldn't see a thing. It was like trying to look through a brick wall. What had I done wrong? I was shocked to think I'd failed on the first try. Why couldn't I work this camera? I examined the gizmos on top, then the viewfinder. I turned the camera around in my hands, looking for the mystery.

And there it was—the lens cap, covering the lens. Now I remembered Aunt Amelia screwing it on, telling me to protect the lens whenever I wasn't using the camera. I took the lens cap off. I put the viewfinder to my eye again, and there was my little world.

I adjusted the blurred image. The picture of Nick came into focus, framed and secure and isolated from everything except the silver brush. There was barely enough light, but when I opened up the f-stop, the light-meter needle centered. I exhaled all my breath to steady the camera, as Aunt Amelia had taught me, and gently pushed the shutter.

As I went through the house making pictures, things seemed to take on more life in the viewfinder than they had as objects. The telephone became a mysterious black shape, full of promise and mystery. I made a jaunty stack of the tapes Nick had given me, while songs tumbled through my head. I photographed the books I pretended to read when we sneaked off together to the amphitheater. I took pictures of the thick, sheltering sycamore tree where Nick propped his bicycle outside our house; the steps we would sit on when he came over, trying not to touch each other because we were exposed to all the neighborhood. I photographed every angle of the Bug, because he loved being driven around in it.

I thought the pictures might make me sad, but they didn't. They all gave me satisfaction.

At three-thirty Susannah came home. I had only two frames left to shoot on the roll of film. An afternoon had never gone so quickly. When I heard her car door slam, I was in the hall fiddling with a close-up of the pattern on my Indian-print skirt—Nick's favorite—under the bright light of the Chinese table lamp. I grabbed my skirt and the camera and raced upstairs. I jammed them in my closet floor, picked up a book, and flopped onto my bed.

I hadn't seen her since last night.

"Hi, dearie," Susannah said, as though everything was normal as pie. "When on earth is this heat wave going to end?" She pulled her hair off her neck and twisted it behind her head. She flapped her elbows as though that might stir up a breeze. "Next summer, I promise you, we're going to get this entire house rewired and air-conditioned. It galls me that Amelia's the only one who lives in comfort."

I didn't show it, but a shock went through me when she said Aunt Amelia's name.

"Any calls?" she asked.

"Mrs. Coatswaddle . . ."

"Coatsworth," she corrected.

". . . saying she'll be able to come to the tea next week. That's it."

She turned to go downstairs. "Mrs. Coatsworth is from one of the oldest families in St. Louis. Beer. Or shoes, maybe." She stopped near the door and straightened a print that was the tiniest bit crooked on the wall. "There. And I bought scallops for dinner."

"Scallops? Great," I faked a yawn. She suspected

nothing, she knew nothing. As far as Susannah was concerned, I'd gone to bed early the night before and hung out all day alone, reading.

"You could poach them in wine and herbs, or just steam them," she said, on her way down the stairs.

I realized what she'd said. *I* could poach or steam them. It was my night to cook.

I leaped from the bed and ran out into the hall. "Susannah, I've got a big favor to ask. Please, please, please say yes."

"Yes to what?" Her voice was full of suspicion.

"Can we trade nights? I'll cook tomorrow, but I really need tonight off."

"Neela, I've been tramping through a hot, dusty barn all afternoon, looking at dirty furniture and trying to talk a farmer into selling it. I really need some time to unwind."

"Please, Susannah," I begged. "This just came up at the last moment."

She studied me for several seconds, then exhaled a long, weary breath. "All right, sweetie. I remember what it was like when I was your age. If you want to have dinner with Nick, go ahead. Just don't ever say I never do anything for you."

Cocktail time had been going on for a while. Liver, Bacon, and Onions scrambled around downstairs, knocking into furniture, the sounds of their mischief funneling up through my open door. "Heel, King!" Leonard's voice rapped out, "Heel and sit!" Then I could hear Leonard and Susannah murmuring to each other. Sometimes, when their voices got quiet and intense, I would sneak halfway down the steps trying to listen, full of dread that they were discussing me. I always wanted to eavesdrop and hated what was being said. It drove me nuts to hear myself referred to as "*she*," as in, "I don't know why she's behaving like that," or, "When is she going to grow up?"

I turned the other way instead. The wide, gray canvas camera strap was firmly over my shoulder as I climbed the stairs to Aunt Amelia's. Her door was ajar; I peeked in, not sure if she'd left it open for me. I could see Aunt Amelia's profile in her chair, like a silhouette against the bare wall, rocking in strong pitches forward and back. It wasn't the comforting rock of an old lady, but full of agitation. I felt as though I were snooping, so I retreated and knocked.

"Yes, yes, it's open," Aunt Amelia called. When she saw me she slammed the brakes on her rocking. "Well? How did it go?"

I perched on the edge of the soft leather couch and told her about the lens cap. She laughed: there were no fangs. "I've done that dozens of times myself," she admitted.

I asked her the questions I'd had about bright sunlight and the shutter speed, amazing myself that such words could come so easily from my mouth. I told her that I was worried that my focus wasn't always accurate.

"A mere technicality," she said, throttling forward in her chair again. "That will come. The important question is: Do you like the pictures you took?"

"I'll have to see how they came out," I answered cautiously.

She gave herself a vigorous push back in her chair. "Are they the ones you wanted to take?"

"I think so," I said, not quite understanding the question.

"Well," she halted on her forward rock and fixed me with a stare. "Did you enjoy taking them?"

That one I could answer with enthusiasm. I loved taking pictures.

"Then let's go in the darkroom and see what your negatives look like."

Aunt Amelia had given me black-and-white film because I'd told her that's what I liked when I was groping for an "artistic" phrase that would interest her in me. And it was true, I did like black-and-white, but not for the reason I'd said. Color film had to be developed by a lab. That meant other people would handle it and might see the prints. I knew from *The Guardian* I could develop black and white myself. The pictures I took were mine. I wanted them private.

I couldn't imagine where to begin in the darkroom. It looked so cozy when I first saw it, and I'd been impressed with all the brown bottles and jars. But now that I faced actually having to use it, those bottles and jars seemed full of poisons and explosives.

Aunt Amelia moved around the little space with calm and assurance. She assembled a small array of equipment and tools on the counter: a bottle opener, scissors, and a developing tank. She gave me a long strip of exposed, discarded film, for practice. Then she held up a plastic reel that reminded me of Leonard's fly-fishing reels but was much smaller.

"And now, the hard part. Learning to get the film on the reel," she announced.

It wasn't so hard. On the second try, I guided the film into the slots and wound it on the reel.

"Good," Aunt Amelia said. "Now do it with your eyes shut."

I did, and it was harder.

"And now, the hard part," she said.

"You've already said that, Aunt Amelia."

"So I have. Enough practice. Here's the real thing." She flicked off the light switch.

The room went blind black. I waited for my eyes to grow accustomed to the darkness, and the black only got thicker. I didn't dare take a step in any direction. There were no cracks of light to guide me.

"I'm right here." Aunt Amelia's voice came velvet smooth next to my shoulder, low and calm. "And your film and the equipment are right in front of you."

I groped for the film on the counter. As I struggled to pry off the film canister top with the bottle opener, the darkroom walls seemed to slam in on me. I felt as though I were living the Edgar Allan Poe story "The Pit and the Pendulum." They closed in further as I freed three feet of my precious exposed film from the canister. The film was springy from being wound up and jumped around like the Slinky I had when I was a kid. It was totally unmanageable. I was terrified I would put my fingers on it. I was terrified I would drop it. I knew I'd never get it onto the reel, even though I'd practiced.

Aunt Amelia made cooing, encouraging noises. I couldn't translate them into English.

At last, the walls just inches from crushing me, with little air left to breathe, I got the film on the reel. Got the reel in the developing tank. Screwed the lid on the tank.

"Nothing to it," said Aunt Amelia as she flicked on the lights. The walls jumped back to where they'd been.

"Piece of cake," I said, and realized I was starved.

"Later," Aunt Amelia said. "First we develop the film."

We mixed chemicals; first, developer, slowly stirring a powder into hot water. We measured fixer into a graduated container—like the ones we used in the science lab at school—and brought it down to sixty-eight degrees. We prepared a stop bath; the smell of acetic acid prickled the inside of my nose. I took notes. It was exacting work, and I wanted to get it absolutely right. Then we developed the film, with all the lights on because it was sealed in a light-proof developing tank. We poured and agitated and timed each process. At last we took out the reel with my film on it and transferred it to a clear plastic washing tank.

"Twenty minutes," Aunt Amelia said, over the bubbling noise of the water. "Meanwhile, we clean up."

I couldn't imagine why it would take so long to rinse the residue from the film, but Aunt Amelia insisted every second was necessary. Each time I checked the big timer above the sink, it had only clicked down by a minute or two. Twenty minutes seemed forever. At last I was able to take the film from the reel, holding it carefully at one end. I was going to see the negatives that would be pictures about Nick.

There were tiny frames on the film, but to my disappointment I couldn't read what was on each one. The values were reversed—dark areas were clear, while light areas were a silvery-black.

"The film hangs here to dry," Aunt Amelia said, clipping it by a clothespin to a wire that ran the width of the darkroom.

"But I've got to see what I did!" I exploded.

"Patience, dear. Patience."

She had no idea how important these photographs were to me.

"Now, about that piece of cake," she said.

Aunt Amelia made us each a tuna-fish sandwich. She didn't chop in onions or celery or red peppers, the way I'd learned, just glopped in the mayonnaise. It was delicious. We finished off with blueberry coffee cake from the supermarket. I thanked her for supper and the developing lesson. She smiled. "Tomorrow morning, eight-thirty," she said as I left.

I was back in my room when the phone rang.

"Hello?" Leonard and I both said, picking up our extensions at the same time.

"Neela?" It was Nick.

I was shocked by his voice. I'd almost forgotten about him for two hours. "I've got it, Leonard," I said desperately.

"You're back? I thought you were out." Leonard said.

"No, I'm here. It's OK, the phone's for me. You can hang up. Nick?"

"No more than three minutes, please," Leonard said. "I'm expecting a call." The phone clicked.

"Neela?" Nick asked again.

"Hi." It was all I could manage to get out.

"Hi." There was silence from him too. "Well. How's it going?"

Just dandy, thank you. Tons of fun. A piece of cake. "OK. How about you?"

"OK. Pretty good. There's a lot going on."

"Like what?" I asked.

"Do you want to see?"

"See what?"

"Hang on, I'll be right over. Meet me on your steps. Ten minutes."

My hand trembled as I hung up. I ran in the bathroom and turned on the shower. There wasn't time to shave my legs or wash my hair. I brushed my teeth. My Indian skirt was still wadded in a ball on my closet floor. I grabbed my silver hairbrush, bent over, and brushed my hair upside down.

Nick wants to see me. Nick wants to show me something.

I ran down the stairs, though it occurred to me to slide down the banister, I felt so happy. I walked quickly through the hall. But not quickly enough.

"Slow down there, girl." Leonard's hand on my shoulder stopped my forward motion. "Where are you going?"

"Just outside on the steps."

"What's going on here?" he asked. "Susannah told me you'd gone out tonight with that boyfriend of yours and couldn't make dinner."

"I couldn't. But I'm just going out now." I tried to breeze by, but his fingers tightened on my shoulder.

"This doesn't make sense. It's nine o'clock at night."

"Have you had dinner yet?" I asked.

"Susannah's in the kitchen putting it on. That's not the point."

"But it is, Leonard," I said desperately. "I couldn't have cooked and gone out, too." I kissed his cheek. "I'll make a fabulous supper tomorrow, I promise." This time I did breeze by. I went out to sit on the steps, the same steps I'd photographed six hours earlier.

132

There was no wind blowing on Arlington Place that night, and every sound seemed intensified in the stillness. When a horn honked on the boulevard, or the traffic swelled, the noise seemed to be originating just feet away. A cat squalled for a mate in the alley behind the houses. The dogs in the kennel got off a few little yaps. Otherwise, it was deadly still, deadly waiting. The neighborhood baseball games had broken up; the skateboards and bikes had been put away. I looked down toward Penelope's house.

It was irrational, but I felt that if I concentrated enough I could make Nick come quickly. He must be borrowing a car to even talk about making it over here in ten minutes. And then I thought: What if someone else is driving him? What if it's Bertie? And the thought was too terrible to allow it to more than flick through my consciousness. Ten minutes had long passed. I sat there counting car headlights on the boulevard, trying to will one to turn up Arlington Place.

Headlights appeared through the open gates. They came larger toward me, jiggling over the first speed bump, then the second and the third. I could see that they were higher and spaced more widely than most cars—a pickup truck, or a van. Two houses away, they slid into the space behind Leonard's car. Nick.

My stomach twisted in on itself. I couldn't get up to go to him. I'd have to stay stuck on the steps until he came over, until I could see if he was alone.

The door slammed. I waited with my eyes screwed shut, my cheeks and face tightened for the sound of a second slam. But all I heard was the jingle of keys hitting the change in Nick's pocket, and the soft shuffle of his shoes on the sidewalk. I popped my eyes open and saw his face in the street light as he came toward me. He was smiling and looking directly at me. It seemed as though nothing at all had happened between us. We were back together as we'd always been.

He held out his hand—not his right, as though he wanted to shake, but his left, palm turned up, waiting for mine. I stood up, but that was as far as I could get. I wanted with every inch of me to take his hand. I felt how his arms would feel around my waist. I saw the place on his shoulder, close to his neck, where my head would lie. And I couldn't move.

"Neela," he said, his voice soft.

"Whose car did you borrow?" I asked.

The moment I heard my voice, I knew I'd broken the spell. Nick's hand pulled back and went in his pocket. The smile that had looked so intimate suddenly turned larger, more general, as though he were smiling at an entire audience. I couldn't imagine why I'd asked that question. I wanted to remake the movie—"take two."

Nick stood on the sidewalk and looked up at me on the steps. He didn't come closer. "That's why I came over. I thought you'd want to see it."

My legs unlocked, and I moved toward him. But he'd already turned his back to me, and was walking out of the street light. There was just enough light to see a small, red, well-used pickup parked beyond Leonard's car.

"Isn't it a beauty." Nick didn't ask a question, he made an irrefutable statement. He ran his hand across the door and let it trail on the hood. "It's mine."

"Yours?" *That's what he said, it was his.* I was stalling for time again, trying to gather my feelings so they

134

wouldn't roll out in the street, like a kicked-over basket of lemons.

"I got it today."

"But what about your bike?" I cried. *Now you can get around without me. Now you don't need me and the Bug. Now you can take other people with you.*

"I've still got my bike, Neela." The way he tacked my name on the end of the sentence told me he'd heard what I really thought. "In fact, I can throw it in the back and go places I've never been able to get to before."

I couldn't stop being the Inquisition. "Why did you get a truck?" *Considering the size of the cab, he might as well have bought a sports car. He could only get one other person, two at the most, in the front seat. It wasn't as though he was going to carry a whole bunch of people with him. Not the band, for instance. Just one person. Just Bertie.*

"Show a little enthusiasm." Now he sounded irritated. "I thought you'd think it was neat. That's why I wanted you to see it."

"I do. I think it's fabulous." My voice was strained.

"Mom helped me pay for it. I'm going to clean some old stuff out of the attic for her, and lay in a couple of cords of fireplace wood for the winter."

I could see Bertie, the ever-ready pal and helpmate raring to help him stack logs, breathless to stretch out in front of the fireplace with him.

"That's the neat thing about a pickup—it's useful. It was a good deal, too—a hundred thousand miles on it, but not much rust."

I didn't hear anything he said; I just thought about Bertie riding next to him.

The cat yowled again from the alley.

"Aw, shut up you shtupid bird . . ."

It was the raw, spittle-coated voice of Mr. Potter. He was right behind me, weaving down the sidewalk. I crouched between Leonard's car and Nick's truck, duck-walking through the space to the street. But Nick stayed right where he was, and from the way he pressed his lips together, I could tell that he was trying to keep from laughing. He wasn't afraid at all. He looked ready to strike up a conversation.

"Outta my way, outta my way," Mr. Potter muttered as he stumbled by.

"Whoa, poor old guy's in terrible shape," Nick said, following Mr. Potter's back with his eyes. "I can't believe his body can take that abuse every night. He's trashed all the time isn't he, Neela?"

I was trembling.

"Neela?"

I wanted to answer Nick, but I couldn't. It had been just a few weeks ago I thought Mr. Potter was a benign, silly old drunk, someone Penelope and I could joke about and call "Mr. Potted," or "Mr. Plastered." He'd seemed so harmless all my childhood, and now I had to close my window every night, even in the heat, to keep his noise from invading my dreams.

I walked toward the steps. I wanted Nick to follow me, to sit with me and keep me safe. But I couldn't ask him, and I couldn't look around. The cat screeched out from the alley again, and this time the dogs set up a chorus of growls and barks in warning. I reached the steps.

I heard Nick's breath behind me as he ran toward me. He caught my arm, but I didn't turn to him. "I have no idea what's going on here," he said, his voice sharp. "But whatever it is, I can't deal with it."

The door slammed. The motor started on his truck. I heard him pull out with a screech of the steering wheel. He turned around by the closed gates and headed toward the open gates of Arlington Place, accelerating past our house. I wanted to run into the street, to pound on his door, to get in beside him. Instead, I kept walking up the steps to our front door.

It wouldn't budge. I looked up. On the other side of the screen was Leonard, holding the door closed.

"And which of your friends was that, may I ask, driving like a maniac on our block?" Leonard kept the door tight shut.

I looked behind me, hoping I'd see the taillights of the truck, but the street was empty. "Let me in," I cried, barely in control.

"Who was that? I want the name. The nerve of him setting the dogs off . . ."

"*He* didn't get the dogs going. It was some dumb cat in the alley."

"Don't tell me, young lady. Anyone that takes off at that speed should be arrested."

"Leonard, please, let me in." I felt sobs beginning in my shoulders. I rattled the door, turning and yanking as hard as I could.

"Tell me who it was." The door held firm.

"Nick!" I whispered.

One word, and the door was open.

EIGHT

Aunt Amelia claimed that four hours each night was plenty of sleep for her. It wasn't nearly enough for me—but I was learning to make do on less. Two things were getting in the way: the number of late hours I spent in Aunt Amelia's darkroom, and the terrible, aching thoughts and memories of Nick that kept me awake, even when I went to bed exhausted. The only time I wasn't actively thinking about him, planning ways to get him back, scheming how to get even with Bertie, I was in the darkroom.

Every morning for the next week, I endured bog-brew breakfasts with Leonard, trying to act normal while he busied himself around the kitchen frying bacon and scrambling eggs with cheese, then standing over me to gauge my reaction to his culinary efforts. I was so dragged out I could hardly swallow. Sometimes his early-morning cheerfulness made me frantic, though usually by the end of breakfast the newspaper had depressed him sufficiently so that he was recognizable as the same old Leonard. When at last he headed off for work, I went up to develop film.

138

In the afternoons, while Susannah was out, I took photographs around the house. I made arrangements of Leonard's fishing equipment, placing his flies artfully in a circle on a background of white paper; I photographed close-ups of the delicate patterns on Susannah's china plate collection. Sometimes, in the afternoon, Susannah would be at home selling antiques; then I stole quietly out into Arlington Place with my camera. I never ventured off the block. I sneaked around photographing any old thing—Liver, Bacon, and Onions snoozing in their kennel, framed by the links in the fence; the Steiner boys, bedecked in white-framed shades and oversized surfers' shirts, doing skateboard tricks; Penelope's empty bedroom window. I tried to avoid pictures that had anything to do with Nick, but it was hopeless. Everything was saturated with reminders of him. Only the darkroom was safe.

In the evenings Aunt Amelia taught me to make prints from my negatives. I'd have to wait until dinner was over to go upstairs, which usually meant nine-thirty or ten, unless I'd been the cook. Several blessed nights they went out to dinner. Then I could eat a tuna sandwich with Aunt Amelia.

I'd set up trays of developer, stop bath, and fixer in the long darkroom sink. Under a deep red safelight, which lent a dim ruby glow to the darkroom, I'd process my prints.

Aunt Amelia supervised my printing at first, keeping a close eye on each stage of the process, and giving advice. Her suggestions were all technical: "Use a number four filter to bring out the whites of clouds"; or, "After the negative is in the enlarger, clean off dust spots with a little brush"; or, "Leave the paper in the developer longer to make the black tones richer." I didn't mind if Aunt Amelia saw these beginner's attempts; I was grateful for every bit of information. It was all practice, every print. I concentrated with all my being, because I knew what it was for. I was clear about what I intended to prove, and this was only the dress rehearsal.

One night—after midnight—my prints were hung to dry, the trays stored under the sink, the safelight turned off, the cap on the enlarger lens. My final chore was to scrub the sink.

"Come have a brownie," Aunt Amelia called, her voice filtering into the darkroom.

"I can't," I moaned. "Susannah says you get fat if you eat right before you go to bed, and I know it's true." I opened the door, and there she was facing me, with a plate of brownies in one hand and a pot of tea in the other.

"Nonsense, and what's a lovely girl like you doing worrying about fat, anyway?" She put the brownie plate down on the glass table. "Now, sit—" She nodded at the rocking chair—"and eat." Smoothing her dress behind her, she settled in the center of the couch.

"But that's your chair."

"It's the best chair for thinking," she said.

"I don't want to think," I said, but I sat on the caned seat of the chair and pushed back with my feet, rocking gently. Almost immediately I felt relief in my weary legs. I found myself munching a brownie. The room looked different from this perspective.

"Why don't you have any of your photographs up on the walls?" I asked Aunt Amelia idly.

"Because it's old work, that's why," she said. "I did it a thousand years ago."

140

"And you don't like your old work?" I ate the last bite of my brownie, and picked a few crumbs off my lap.

"I was satisfied with it once."

"Remember all those boxes you had in your bedroom?" The rocking seemed to make me persist.

"I'm not likely to forget them." She spoke with her teeth clamped together, lips barely moving.

"I saw a photograph in the top box once, and I thought—"

"You do too much thinking. I don't mean to sound unkind, but that's work I no longer want anyone to see. Anyone."

I didn't know what to say, so I took a second brownie off the plate.

"Let's talk about *your* work, Neela. Are you happy with the pictures you're taking?"

"You asked me that once before." I didn't want to answer. I wasn't happy with anything.

"Well?"

"I like doing the darkroom stuff. But . . ."

"But you're not taking the pictures you really want to take."

"Not exactly." I tried to keep my answer neutral.

"You had something else in mind when you started all this."

I felt as though my skin were peeling off and bones were melting. Everything vital was exposed. She couldn't know, but she did. I'd never mentioned Nick's name, but she knew.

"Sort of," I shrugged.

"Well then, move," she said, jumping up. I watched her stride to the apartment door, as though she expected me to be only a step behind. "Get on with it." She flung the door open. "Go to bed, and tomorrow start taking pictures from your heart. You have to do it, you know."

I hated those abrupt changes in her; I didn't know what to make of her leaping from sweet to sour and back again. But she was right. It was time.

My blue nylon backpack was crammed with books and homework during the school year, but empty now. In the outside pouch I put my driver's license, some money, and the Swiss army knife Leonard had given me one Christmas. In the main compartment, I made a nest for the camera. Most people carried their camera in a case, but mine was going out bare into the world: Aunt Amelia said cases were only for people who didn't need their camera ready at all times. The camera needed protection and needed to remain concealed. When I'd taken pictures on Arlington Place, I'd practiced trying to be invisible, sheltering the camera with my hands when I wasn't actually taking a picture, and slinking around. Now it was crucial: The camera and I must not be seen.

I carried the backpack downstairs and put it under the hall table so I could make a speedy exit the minute dinner was over. Susannah played endlessly with her goat cheese and sun-dried tomato salad, separating out little bites with her fork, then never getting them to her mouth. Leonard ate helping after helping of frittata, saying, "Just one more little sliver." They filled wine glasses and refilled them. Dinner was endless. I said I didn't want any raspberry sorbet because I was late meeting a friend. They bought that.

I drove to Nick's neighborhood. My heart beat so violently I could feel it pulsing in my throat and wrists. When I approached his driveway, I slowed almost to a stop. It was dark; there were no street lights. I peered down the drive, but I couldn't see anything except a luminous glow from behind his house. *The garage. The band.* I crept on, leaving his wooded lane and turning into the next subdivision. I parked by the junction of the road, praying no one would think it odd that a car had been abandoned in such an unlikely place. The peepers and crickets were serenading each other when I got out of the Bug. The backpack was firm on my shoulders.

There was a shortcut to Nick's house through the backyards and woods, but I didn't dare take it. It went by Bertie's house. It was too easy to imagine automatic sentry lights popping on and her parents dialing the police. I would have to chance the road. The moon wasn't visible yet, but there were clusters of lights from houses, and the white line that edged the road guided me, like an unwound ball of twine leading to Nick's.

A car came toward me. I stepped well off the road and ducked my head as it drew near. Even though it passed me, I watched for the brake lights to go on. In this suburb no one walked along the road at night alone. *If that happens again I've got to hide.*

I tiptoed down Nick's driveway, each crunch of the gravel sounding like an explosion. His red pickup was parked in the driveway turnout, its wheels turned sharply, as though he'd skidded in and leapt from the truck. Wolf Man's car was there also. To my relief, Mrs. Cunningham's gray Nissan was gone. The house was dark.

The garage lights were a beacon as I crept along the hedge that separated it from the house. Everything was oddly quiet for a band rehearsal. I stopped and listened intently for the low muffle of men's voices and Bertie's higher one. I looked around carefully at the dark shadows, then dashed across the small lawn to the safety of the garage wall. That little sprint, which would have been nothing in the real world, left my breath rasping in my throat.

The garage window was right above me. It was closed, as the windows and doors had to be when they were practicing, to keep the neighbors from complaining. I stayed crouched another minute while I got the camera from my backpack, then slowly straightened my legs to three-quarters position so I could point the lens at the bottom of the garage window. Whatever was going on in there, I needed a photo of it.

Nick, Wolf Man, and the keyboard player were all clustered around their instruments. Nick was sitting on a stool, tuning his guitar. *Nick, my wonderful Nick.* I turned the zoom so his upper body was in the viewfinder, shoulder pulled up, head bent, ear close to his guitar strings. My finger was on the shutter button before I realized the light-meter needle wasn't centered. I brought the camera down and checked the shutter speed by the light of the window, praying Nick would stay just where he was. And when the camera was ready and at my eye again, Nick was still tuning up. The *click* of the shutter was the loudest sound in the night.

There was a rustle from the driveway and I froze. I could hear the garage door opening and voices calling out into the night.

"Yo, Bertie!"

"Where've you been?"

"Sorry, guys, my mom wanted me . . ."

The door shut, the voices faded, and I was left with my window to spy through, as though sound had been shut off in a movie.

I looked through the camera. There was Nick, *horrible, hateful, deceiving Nick*, his hand on Bertie's shoulder, pushing her to the center of the room. Oh, this was what I wanted. This was what I'd risked so much to get. I knew he was going out with her, I just hadn't been able to prove it before. Now here it was on film, and I could see for myself that I hadn't just been making up these feelings that began with her name and ended in my twisted gut. *Focus.* They were smiling at each other. *Click.* She put her hand on his guitar. *Focus. Click.* They read something together, her hair falling against her cheek. *Focus. Click. Click. Click.*

I stopped when I'd shot the whole roll. The instant I brought the camera away from my eye, I felt defenseless and terrified. They could come out of the garage at any moment. I'd put myself at terrible risk. I stuffed the camera in the backpack, and keeping low, ran along the hedge.

Lights were on in the kitchen; Mrs. Cunningham was back. I stretched up so I could see in the window, and there she was at the kitchen table, eating her nightly yogurt and reading a book. I watched her for a moment, while she did nothing more than raise her spoon and turn a page. How I longed to go in, to throw myself in the empty chair and beg her to tell me what I was doing. She would take off her reading glasses and pour me a glass of iced tea. She might give me a hug. She would comfort me, help extract me from this feverish need to know everything and prove how Nick had betrayed me. She would say I was hurting myself, and I didn't need to do it, that I could stop anytime I wanted. But I couldn't. The hurt felt too familiar. I'd known it forever. It was old and deep, almost comfortable, as though I were coming home.

I skipped breakfast with Leonard and went straight up to Aunt Amelia's with my film. She didn't answer my knock. I knew I was early, I knew I should go down and wait until eight-thirty, but I also knew she kept her key on the transom above the door. It was too tempting. Aunt Amelia had a good four inches on me in height, so I had to make little jumps to feel for it. At last my fingers hit the key; one more jump and it was in my hand. I put it in the lock and turned.

It was only when the door opened into the empty room that I began to feel strange—after all, wasn't this breaking and entering? I hadn't been alone in the room since Aunt Amelia moved in, and the shape of it—the way the eaves sloped down to protect the windows—made me feel once again that this was where I belonged. True, it no longer resembled my dusty, abandoned hideaway, but it was still the best place in the house.

"Aunt Amelia?" I called tentatively.

Nothing.

As I went toward the darkroom, I heard the raining sound of the shower coming from the bathroom. In a minute the shower stopped, and I knocked gently on the door.

"Good Lord, what's going on?" There was genuine alarm in her voice.

"Nothing, Aunt Amelia, it's just me," I called, my lips almost on the door. "Neela."

"Is something wrong? Aren't you early? And how did you—" she swung open the door—"get in?"

Her scrubbed face was inches from mine. Without make-up she looked younger, babyish even, with a natural kind of pinkness. Gone were the circles of red that flamed from her cheeks, and fussy little brows appeared where the heavy brown pencil usually crooked above her eyes. A long terrycloth robe covered her, and a turban-towel was twisted on her head. She smelled of shampoo and soap.

"I'm sorry, Aunt Amelia. I just *have* to, I really *have* to use the darkroom right away."

"Well, that's enthusiasm for you. All right. But how did you get in? Did I leave the door unlocked?"

I think I blushed. "I remembered where you hid the key."

"Hum." She considered things. "Not much of a hiding place, I guess. Just as well. You go ahead now while I get my face on." She started to shut the door.

"You don't need to put a face on for me," I said. I didn't know where that came from.

"I'll put my face on where and when I like," she said, frowning.

"I just mean, I like you any way you are." I didn't know where that came from, either.

In the darkroom I took the developing tank and reel from the shelves. I made sure the door was well shut and light tight and my tools for loading film were placed in the proper order on the counter in front of me. By now when I turned off the lights I no longer panicked.

An hour later my negatives were drying and I'd set up the trays for making prints. My insides were fluttering with fear or excitement, I couldn't tell which. On some level I was rather proud of what I'd done last night: It took true nerve to spy on Nick as I had. On the other hand, it wasn't really nerve that drove me, but something deeper, something out of control. In the darkroom I could make it seem more reasonable; after all, Aunt Amelia had practically ordered me to take the kind of pictures I really wanted to take. But I was shocked by my feelings just the same. Here I was, trembling to see Nick's face—not his face as he'd sat alone on the stool with his guitar, but his face at the moment he touched Bertie's arm. If I'd begun this trip taking pictures because I wanted to build a little shrine to him, things had certainly changed. Now all I wanted was to examine the proof that he loved someone else.

"Neela!" This time it was Aunt Amelia knocking on my door. I didn't want her in here. She'd taught me everything I'd learned, but it was too shameful to think of her seeing these pictures.

"Neela!" She rattled the door. I opened. She had her "face" on, make-up slathered over her wrinkles, eyebrows settled firmly, lipstick outlining a new mouth. Her eyes were full of warning. "Susannah's here. She wants to talk to you."

She closed the door and went back into the sitting room, leaving me. I'd been discovered.

"Well my goodness, haven't you fixed this up nicely since the last time I was here," I could hear Susannah coo.

I put my hand to my throat, feeling my pulse every-where, in my neck, in my thumbs, in my temples. I couldn't bear it that Susannah had found me. There was no safe place left.

"A little sparse," her voice continued, "but that can always be fixed. I have a few exceptionally fine pieces downstairs you might take a look at, Amelia."

Trying to look confident and nonchalant, I sauntered into the sitting room.

"Good morning, sweetie-pie." Susannah's voice lost none of its slipperiness. "Imagine finding you here."

"Hi, Susannah." I had to say something that would betray none of my anxiety. "Isn't this a little early for you?"

"Early? No, indeedy. You've no doubt forgotten what today is." Susannah settled a half smile on me, one that said, *Please don't be so thick.*

Today? Today I see the pictures of Nick and Bertie. I glanced over at Aunt Amelia. She had turned discreetly away while we talked but was rubbing her palms together as though she were cold or were hatching a plan.

"Tea, dear. Tea. Tea. And I could use some help getting set up. I know you made cookies yesterday, but there's still quite a lot to do. So if you'll kindly follow me downstairs . . ."

"Susannah," Aunt Amelia interrupted. "I'd like to keep Neela up here with me a little while longer. She's in the middle of helping me sort out some things." Aunt Amelia had grown another six inches. She looked down over a long upper lip and prominent chin. "She'll be along shortly to give you a hand."

Without anything else being said, she hustled Susan-nah out the door and redirected me toward the darkroom.

149

•   •   •

"Well, that took some nerve," Susannah proclaimed when I came into the pantry half an hour later. Newspaper had been spread on the table, which was piled with silver teapots, creamers, sugar bowls, platters, and teaspoons. "Amelia certainly can be bossy."

I wiped my damp hands on the sides of my shorts. My contact sheet was drying upstairs in the darkroom, each tiny, negative-sized image of Nick and Bertie lined up next to another, as though they were cartoon frames. The developer tray had been covered with plastic wrap, so it wouldn't go bad in the hours before I could return to make more prints.

"Help yourself to a teapot and some silver polish," she said. "I've done most of it, but I've saved some for you." She paused. "What were you doing in her apartment, anyway?"

"Pickle jars," I answered decisively.

"I assume this was your first time up there," she said, without questioning the nonsense that had just come from my mouth.

I stayed quiet.

"She's a very depressed old lady. I'm not sure it's good for you to be around her."

"What do you mean, 'depressed'?" I dipped a square of flannel in the polish and began rubbing a spout.

"She never goes anywhere. She doesn't like a soul. That's a true sign of depression."

"How do you know she doesn't like anyone?" I kept my eyes down, my hand very busy polishing the handle.

"It's obvious. I've asked her down for cocktails

countless times and she's never come. And yesterday I called to invite her to the tea this afternoon. She was polite enough, but said she didn't think she'd be able to make it."

"Maybe Mrs. Coatswaddle—"

"Coatsworth."

"And Mrs. Diddlyquack just aren't her kind of people."

"Your little jokes fail to amuse me. Emily Coatsworth and even Bertha Babcock—though she can be a pain in the nuisance—are the finest St. Louis has to offer. Amelia would benefit from their company."

The doorbell chimed, and from the back the dogs started a minor ruckus.

"The florist," Susannah cried triumphantly, jumping up from the table. I finished a creamer and gave the teaspoons a quick once-over. Susannah returned with an enormous oblong box. She opened it, and the green tissue-paper lining crinkled as she peeled it back. There was a garden of reds and yellows and blues, all on long stems. *Mrs. Cunningham's garden.* She pulled vases from the cupboard, and began to arrange the flowers.

"Is that all you need from me?" I asked.

"One more thing. Put the Belgian lace cloth on one of the dining-room tables. No, wait—I'd better not cover it up, since Margaret Zipperman is interested in a Queen Anne reproduction table. Just arrange the silver nicely, and then you can go."

I went into the dining room and began to set the tea table. I'd done this before.

"Don't forget to spread the spoons in a fan shape. It looks so much more elegant," she called. "Oh, I forgot to give you a message. While you were helping Amelia, Penelope called. She's home."

Home? I jogged down Arlington Place, the Radfords' house bouncing nearer with each step. *How could Penelope have gotten home so soon? Was this when she said she'd be back? Then where had all the days gone?*

While I waited for a response to my two-ring doorbell signal, I used the shined, brass door knocker as a mirror. The image of my face was both fuzzy and distorted— my nose long as Pinocchio's. At last Mrs. Radford answered, and after only a minute of conversation about which colleges I was going to apply to and how the summer had gone, I was free to run up the stairs. I planned to blaze into Penelope's room, whooping and screaming with joy that she was home.

But at her shut door I suddenly felt shy. For the first time ever, and without knowing why, I knocked.

"Come on in, Mom," Penelope yelled.

I opened the door and stood there, staring at Penelope and soaking in her amazed stare. I touched my nose to make sure it was the normal length. "Well?" I said.

"Well, look folks, it's not Mom. Hi there, number-one friend," Penelope said, and then we were hugging. *She's back, she's really back.*

"Camp was fabulous?" I asked.

"The best."

"Who gave you the haircut?" I asked with admiration. The ponytail Penelope had always worn was gone, and newly released curls framed her face.

"You like it?" She shook her head to set the curls in motion.

"You look great, Pen. Penelope," I corrected myself. Sometimes the urge to shorten her name into something more affectionate was overwhelming.

Her room was different somehow, but I couldn't figure out what it was at first. None of her furniture had been sold. More blue ribbons were crowded on the wire stretched across her wall—but that was to be expected after a month of competing in horse shows. There was a new trophy in her bookcase—a round silver platter, much like the one Susannah was planning to use for tea cookies.

"My God, girl," I said, hitting my forehead with my fist, "it's so clean in here! What happened? I know, I know—the airline lost all your clothes."

"Nope." She grinned in satisfaction. "As a matter of fact, I'm a reformed character." She swept open her closet door. Shoes were neatly lined up. Clothes hung on hangers.

"I should say you're reformed. I'm impressed— What's going on?"

"I want to hear about your summer, first. Then I'll tell you."

The flutter of nervousness in my throat was beginning to feel chronic. I wanted to tell Penelope everything, but I couldn't imagine starting. "No, you first. Whatever's turned you into a neatnik, I want to hear about it. Now."

"It's simple. I've come to grips with my priorities." Penelope bounced cross-legged on her bed, the same old Penelope. "I've been riding forever, right? But now I'm serious about it."

"You've always been serious."

"Wrong. I've always been crazy about horses, and I've always taken my riding for granted. That's not the same as being serious." By the way she fiddled with a braided bracelet on her arm, I could tell it was hard to look at me. This was important to her.

"What's changed in a mere four weeks?" Oh, how ironic that sounded. *A mere four weeks is a lifetime.*

"I worked really hard at camp. I had a lot of responsibility with the younger kids, so I had to set a decent example. Plus, I really had to stretch myself with my own riding."

"What does that mean?" I sat on her rug and raked my fingers through the "pasture."

"I had to be a lot more disciplined than I ever expected. It was my job to see all the saddles and bridles were kept clean and the tack room was in order." She nodded at the closet and grinned. "That's just one example of my nasty new habits."

"So what else made you serious?" I asked.

"I had to be a lot braver than I knew I was. I made the big leap from show jumping to eventing, which meant I went on some awesome cross-country gallops. The first time, when I walked the course before I rode it, the fences looked enormous and impossible." She jumped up and put her hand to her chest, marking heights up to her forehead. "Some had ditches in front of them, and some were as wide as my bed. I was really scared. But my instructor said I could do it, and she helped me figure out how to ride every fence."

"So you did it and you didn't die."

"Correct. Actually, I loved it."

"Which made you serious."

Penelope blushed, she actually blushed. "OK, that's enough. It's your turn. I got your letter, so let's get to it. What's happening on the home front?"

"Everything's pretty much the same." Words were beginning to feel like fat plugs in my throat.

"What about that aunt of yours who moved in? Is that OK?"

"I don't see much of her. Susannah says she keeps to herself because she's depressed. But she's all right."

"So what's going on with Nick? I really couldn't make out what the scene was from your letter."

We were there. I could lay out all the things I'd fuzzed in the noncommittal note I'd finally sent her— everything—his pulling back, sex, the band, the Bertie Albrecht stuff, getting drunk, his truck. And I wanted to do that. But what I couldn't deal with was the spying part. It was too slimy. And that was the installment I was living now. It was consuming me, eating up my heart and stomach and liver and tongue. So it seemed I couldn't say anything.

"That grim, huh?" Penelope asked, reading my silence.

"Not really. Just kind of depressing."

"It'll help to talk about it." Her voice had dropped into that kind, listening tone that put me on the edge of tears.

"You know how it is." I locked my fingers and stretched my arms above my head. I even managed to yawn. "Boyfriends come and go."

"Hey Neela, it's me, Penelope. Reality check time. I know how important he is to you." She leaned forward, trying to hook my eyes with hers.

"Was. He was important. What's happened this summer is over."

"Yeah, but what happened? Did he start going out with someone else?"

Oh, don't let the name Bertie Albrecht cross her lips. I prayed she'd forgotten that talk we had before she went to camp.

"I don't know what he's up to, but whatever it is, it isn't me. Come on, let's not talk about him anymore." I stood up and went to her bookcase, trying to look purposeful. All the books were neatly aligned, their titles right side up. *Next thing you know she'll put them in alphabetical order.*

She was right behind me. "Neela, you're acting weird."

"I'm not!" I wanted to stamp my foot. "Give it a rest, Penelope. Tell me a joke or something."

She stared at me, and then blew her breath out slowly. "OK. You win. Let's go out and get a hamburger somewhere."

"I can't." I could hear my voice, sullen and deceitful. "Susannah has one of her famous teas this afternoon, and I said I'd help." Actually, Susannah didn't want any help with the event. She liked the teas to appear as though they were happening effortlessly, without the aid of human hand.

"I think my mom's going," Penelope said, swallowing my lie. "As soon as you get sprung, come on over. We'll think of something to do tonight."

"I can't." The words jerked out before she'd finished her sentence. "I've already made some plans." *Oh lies, lies, lies. But Penelope was getting too close to the truth.*

The hurt in her eyes was instant. "Aren't you the social queen of the year. Some new guy? Have fun, Neela."

"I didn't know you were coming home today." That, at least, was the truth.

"Well, call me when you have a moment."

And before I knew it I'd left Penelope in her room and was on the street, walking up to number seven Arlington Place.

NINE

Miniature images of Nick and Bertie glistened on the contact sheet through a surrounding black. I bent over each one with a magnifying glass, examining the shapes of the bodies, the way his arm pressed against hers, the way she leaned toward him when she sang. But I couldn't see the expressions on their faces—the curve of his mouth, the glimmer in her eye. No matter how close I brought the magnifying glass, I could make them no clearer. Still, I circled each frame that looked promising with a red grease pencil.

The first negative was positioned in the negative carrier. With a quick burst of air from a pressurized can, I cleared any remaining dust off the surface. The enlarger light shone down through the film: there were Nick and Bertie, projected on the smooth surface of the easel. I felt such power just bringing them into focus. I could crank the enlarger head up high on the shaft and make them huge, or take it way down and shrink them. I could center them, or push them off to the side. For these few moments they were in my control.

I wanted the expression in their eyes. I took up the enlarger as far as it would go, focused, and slipped in a shiny sheet of paper. I adjusted the aperture setting on the enlarger lens. The ruby-red safelight went off while the timer exposed the print, and I held my breath during those ten seconds. Then I slipped the paper into the developer, and watched the magic as it happened. I rocked the tray to keep the liquid washing evenly over the blank paper, like gentle ocean swells, until the images of Nick and Bertie were there, swimming up to meet me.

But when I'd fished them from the fixer and turned on the overhead light, I saw the print was all wrong. Instead of being smooth and whole, each grain was bloated. The outlines were fuzzy, the tones muddy. The picture didn't tell me much.

So I made a new print, bringing the enlarger head down so that most of the negative was included. This time Nick and Bertie looked fleshy and substantial, so real I felt their skin would indent if I touched it. Bertie's skirt was draped in deeply shadowed folds. Nick's white T-shirt gleamed like a polished pearl. I could see the shine of heat from his neck.

I came out of the darkroom. Five good prints and many rejects, still wet, had been arranged face down on the drying racks. Aunt Amelia waited in her sitting room, clad in the same black, long-sleeved, high-necked dress she wore the time she went out for darkroom supplies. Thick-soled black shoes turned her feet into clodhoppers, and stockings tinted her legs a deadly gray.

"What's up?" I asked, alluding to her clothing, but tactfully not mentioning that she was going to roast—

cook like a spit-turned chicken—the moment she left her air-conditioned apartment.

"What's up is downstairs."

"You mean you're going to Susannah's tea?"

"Amazing as that may seem, yes." She patted her hair in place.

"Why?"

"Because I was invited." She stopped as though considering the real reason. "And I've said 'no' to Susannah too many times. She's going to get the wrong idea about me."

"Somehow you don't seem like the type."

"What type?"

"You know, the antique-tea type."

"It won't hurt me for a couple of hours. Besides, I never know when I might meet a fascinating conversationalist." She dropped me a wink with her mascara-covered eyelashes. "I gather you're not planning to attend this event?"

"Oh no," I said, barely keeping the horror from my voice. "This is Susannah's gig."

"What are your plans, then? More darkroom work?"

"Later, maybe. Right now I think I'll go out for a while."

That statement hung there, unacknowledged. In the silence, I felt the same flood of longing to speak I'd felt at Penelope's earlier. I wanted to tell Aunt Amelia everything. I wanted to show her all the photographs. But I knew I wouldn't. My jealousy was like some greedy little porcupine living inside me. The more I fed it, the more it had to have. I could feel it bulging, bloating, stabbing me with its needles. Every hour was becoming more painful. I wanted to talk about it, but it didn't seem possible that I could.

From the top of the stairs, I heard women arriving for the tea, kissing each other, examining the goods. Antique words like "armoire" and "Chippendale" were flung around. Someone said "canopy," and I feared for my bed.

Liver, Bacon, and Onions weren't barking, but from the kennel I could hear the eager noises they made in their throats, desperately begging to come in and have tea and the cookies I'd made yesterday.

I glanced at the prints of yachts on the landing, longing to pirate one and sail away. As I crept downstairs I hugged the wall, my blue backpack over my shoulder with the camera nested in it. If I went down noiselessly, it was possible I might not be noticed.

No such luck. My foot had barely touched the bottom step when Mrs. Radford zeroed in on me. "Neela!" she called.

I zigzagged my eyes to see if Susannah had spotted me. She was nowhere around, though I thought I heard her laugh echoing from the dining room, like splintered glass tinkling to the ground.

"I know how glad Penelope was to see you this morning," Mrs. Radford gushed. Her voice was higher, louder than usual, and she snapped the clasp of her shoulder bag open and shut as she spoke. "She had such a good time at camp, but of course she missed her friends."

Mrs. Radford and I'd had a chat earlier in the day, when she was herself. What was all this about? Did she know how teed-off Penelope was with me?

"I'm glad she's home, Mrs. Radford," I said, shifting the backpack.

"And you're all set to go out, aren't you dear? Where are you girls off to?" She glanced down at her purse, closing it with a definite twist.

"I've got some stuff to do. . . . It's nice to see you, Mrs. Radford." I backed up to the screened door and felt for the knob behind me. "Enjoy the tea. 'Bye." I retreated out the door, smiling like crazy.

As I rolled over a speed bump, I peered through the windshield of the Bug, up at Penelope's window. The shades had been rolled to the top, a sure sign she was home and trying to get every ray of sun into her room. She was a maniac for light. Then I was past her house, headed for the spiked gates of Arlington Place. Penelope was out of my life again. Nothing else existed. I had to find Nick. I had to see him.

Think, think, think, where is he now? It was Thursday afternoon. One of the days—*or was it Wednesday?*—that Nick worked late. *Thursday, yes.*

I drove to the West County Mall, home of Uncle Sam's. It wasn't a new, self-contained mall, but the old-time sprawling kind. I looked for a parking space and finally found an empty one not blocked by shopping carts. Cashiers' slips and candy wrappers littered the asphalt. I sat in the Bug for a moment, trying to get my bearings, while the smells of ginger and sesame oil wafted into the car from the Chinese restaurant. I'd forgotten to have lunch, and I never missed meals.

I took the backpack from the Bug and began to walk toward Uncle Sam's—not directly through the parking lot, where anyone looking out the music-store window

162

might see me—but along the arcade of stores. Back-to-school clothes and lunch boxes were already being featured in the windows. *How was I going to go back to school without Nick?*

I edged up to Uncle Sam's huge window. It was impossible to see into the store through its album displays and posters and *Lowest Price in Town* banners. There was no way to find out if he was working except by going inside.

"Check your backpack, miss?" a uniformed security man said at the door.

"No," I said, clutching it—and the camera—to me.

"Got to, if you're going in." He dangled a plastic number at eye level, expecting me to hand over the bag.

"Can't I just look around to see if someone's here? I'll only be a second."

"Sure. Just leave the backpack."

At that moment, over the cashier's counter, half hidden by customers, I saw Nick's head. His back was to me, but the way the dark curls licked his neck, the slope of his shoulders, were unmistakable. He was here. He was working as a salesman. *Rock 'n' roll with sex appeal.*

With my back to the guard, I unzipped the backpack. *Can I be arrested for taking photos? No way. What I'm doing is perfectly legal.* It only took a second to frame and focus—*click*—and advance the film for two more shots —*click, click.*

Then I was past the guard, out the door, on the walkway, my heart pounding. Back to the Bug, fast.

I sat rigid in the car, every muscle in my body strained. I had a clear view of Uncle Sam's. I didn't dare leave, even to get anything to eat, though the Chinese food smells were making me dizzy with hunger. The camera was in my hand, braced against the dashboard, pointed at the store. *What do I think I'm doing? Why can't I leave this poor guy, who obviously doesn't want me, alone?* I thought of people I'd read about who believed that taking their picture was stealing their soul. Well, they were right. That's just what I intended to do.

I stayed in the car feeling stupid, and awkward, and at the same time determined that Nick would not come out of that store without me photographing him. Then I remembered the truck. If Nick was here, the truck was probably here. I should have looked for it, rather than exposing myself to all that risk. I could catch him at the truck. I opened the door, hooked my toes on the springy seat-edge, and boosted myself up. Hanging on inside the door frame with one hand, I shaded my eyes with the other. I could see hundreds of cars and a few pickups.

"Yo, Neela."

My own name sent electric jolts up my strained legs. I twisted back and saw Wolf Man peering up at me, his head below my shoulder.

"Whatcha doing, girl? Need any help?"

I struggled to find my voice. "I'm looking for something. Someone. My friend Penelope."

"You look ready to fall off that seat, that's what you look," he said. "Come on down."

I felt his hands close around my waist and lift me up a little as I stepped back and down to the parking lot.

"Well," he said.

"Well," I echoed. It seemed we had nothing to say, so we looked at each other. He was a strange character, though good looking in an odd way. Because his shoulder-length red hair frothed around him like a scarlet halo, he kept it in place with a caplike bandana. He held his head to one side, while his wide smile drew up almost to his opposite ear, as though he were trying to keep himself in balance. His arms were never at rest, but karate chopping the air, throwing a baseball, sword fighting—all the motions of drumming, I suspected.

"So. You're just hanging out waiting for your friend?" He shoved his hands in his pockets to keep them still.

"I'm not sure she's here, actually. She may have gone." All this lying made me look at my turquoise ring, twist it around on my finger.

"So you're just hanging out?" he repeated.

"Kind of."

"You want to go see a movie? There's ten of them starting at five o'clock at the Cineplex-ten." He nodded at the giant billboard by the mall entrance, which listed five different movies on each side.

I stared at him. Was he asking me out, in some weird way?

"The band's meeting in front of the ticket window soon—we're going to decide which one to see."

My mouth went instantly dry. I shook my head before he'd finished speaking. *The band's meeting* was all I needed to hear. "I've got to get home."

"You sure?" His one-sided smile came slowly down. "I thought you were going to hang out for a while."

"I was. But I remembered, I can't." Quickly, I got in the Bug and started the motor.

"Hold it." He jammed his arm straight out, palm to me. "It's a good thing you're sitting down, because you've got your foot so far in your mouth you'd trip if you tried to walk."

"I know," I said miserably.

165

"You're a really bad liar."

I nodded.

"It's OK." His grin crept up to his ear again. "Just to prove what a good guy I am, I'll see you get out of this-here parking lot safely." He ran behind the car and motioned me to back up, beckoning with his hands as though I were in a tight squeeze.

I had to laugh. "I'll see you," I said as I took the gear out of reverse. "'Bye, Wolf—" I jerked forward—"Man."

Before I'd gone ten feet anxiety gripped me. I jammed on the brakes. "Hey," I called out the window. Wolf Man was still looking at the back of the Bug. "Can I ask you a favor?"

"Ask."

"Don't tell anyone—you know, *anyone*—you saw me here. It's really important, OK?"

He shrugged and nodded, and he was still grinning.

I turned out the mall entrance.

A few minutes later, I came back.

This time I was completely on patrol for any of the band. I didn't go near my old parking place. I watched from the car until I saw Wolf Man and Ronnie, the keyboard player, waiting by the ticket booth of the Cineplexten. Even though they were far from me and would be barely recognizable in a picture, I focused the camera and brought them as close as I could. *Click*. Then Bertie arrived, *Alberta Albrecht* as she was identified on class lists and in yearbook sports pictures. *Click*. In my pictures she would be known as Bertie the boyfriend thief.

And then Nick was there, tossing his head and acting happy—*focus, click*—his hand on everyone's shoulders, lingering on Bertie's—*click, click*. They bought their tickets. They disappeared inside the theater.

166

In panic, I ran from the car, the blue knapsack hanging by one shoulder strap. It banged against me as I tore along the arcade, slowing and sideskipping to pass shoppers and baby strollers, braking to avoid a head-on collision with an old man. I ran to the entrance of the huge theater.

I never gave a thought to the woman who stood next to the brass post and velvet rope. "Ticket?" she asked.

Ticket? I turned around. I searched the front pouch of the backpack. Two dollars, another single, and at last a five. Yes, I had enough money. I went back outside to the ticket booth.

There were two people ahead of me. The first man stood at the window for so long, I thought he must be catching up on old times with the ticket seller. When I peered around to see what was going on, I saw huge amounts of change being counted out. The next woman bought five tickets for a group of little kids fidgeting by the "coming next" poster. At last it was my turn.

"Which movie?" the ticket seller asked.

"I don't know yet," I answered. "I'll make up my mind when I get inside."

I'll find them in there. I'll sit behind them and see how they are with each other. I'll watch his arm go around her. I'll catch her head on his shoulder.

"Miss, we don't sell tickets that way." Her voice sounded measured and tiredly patient. "You have to know which movie you're going to, and I'll give you a ticket for that theater."

I stared at her. At first her words were as strange as Russian, then the syllables began to rearrange themselves.

Big tears scratched at my throat and eyes. I turned

away while they splattered down my cheeks and stained my shirt. Slowly, I walked down the arcade.

This was it. This was the end. I didn't know what to do next. All my plotting had turned to nothing but humiliation.

The store windows blurred and swam as I passed them—Flora's Homemade Ice Cream; Gigantic Clearance on All Summer Clothes; Epicure Wine and Liquors; St. Louis Hot Tubs; The Diet Center. I stopped in front of each one and pretended to look. I didn't know what else to do. And then I saw the phone booth.

I ran to it, dropping the backpack on the floor and anchoring it between my feet. I closed the glass door. I dialed home.

I snuffed the tears out of my voice. The phone rang, three, four, five times. I was about to hang up.

"Hello!" Susannah said, her voice a promise of cheerfulness and energy.

"Hi, it's me," I said.

"What? I can barely hear you."

There were light voices and tinkling in the background. The tea. I'd forgotten the tea. "It's me," I said louder, speaking distinctly into the mouthpiece.

"Sweetie! Sweetie, I'm so glad you called!" Then I heard her take her mouth from the phone, and say to the room, "It's Neela—I'll only be a minute."

"Susannah, I really need to talk to you."

"The cookies are lovely! Everyone's enjoying them so much!"

I switched the receiver to my other ear, as though that would make better sense of what she'd just said. "Susannah, Nick and I have broken up. Things are horrible."

"Mrs. Radford says you're the best cookie-baker she knows!"

A strange voice came distantly through the phone. "Absolutely marvelous cookies, Neela!"

"You see?" It was Susannah again.

"Look, I know people are still there, but can't you go upstairs and talk to me for a few minutes?"

"Yes, unfortunately you missed most of them. But Mrs. Coatsworth, Mrs. Babcock, and Mrs. Sykes haven't left yet. And Mrs. Radford, of course. I'll tell them you said hello."

Aunt Amelia. She would understand this. She was the only one. "Is Aunt Amelia there?"

"Amelia? Oh my goodness, she looked wonderful. Everyone said it was so good to see her. She was really the toast of St. Louis in her day, you know." I could imagine Susannah turning to everyone in the room and nodding.

I started to cry again. "I'm in a shopping mall. I don't know what to do."

"Well, don't buy the first thing you try on, is my advice. Be sure it's perfect for the dance."

What dance? I ran my fingers over the telephone dial. If I pressed the buttons, the phone would beep in that odd, musical way.

"Leonard and I are having cocktails at the Fairsteins, then going to The Coach House for dinner, so you may want to stay with your friends since you're having fun."

"OK, I get it. Never mind." There was no hope. She wasn't going to embarrass herself by admitting something could possibly be wrong in front of her clients. I was stranded by myself.

"I'm so glad, darling, and I can't wait to hear about

169

it later. 'Bye, sweetie." She made a kissing noise into the phone before it went dead.

The Bug was my refuge, my haven. Recently it seemed I was always in it when I didn't know where to go. I wasn't returning home—either to the tea remnants, or the empty house. Aunt Amelia was probably there, but I didn't want to hear about how she'd been "the toast of the town." So I sat in the Bug, and looked at the Cineplex-ten, and thought about what movie I'd like to have seen.

Shoppers came out of stores, and new cars were exchanged for old ones on either side of me. I had no idea how much time had passed. A green-yellow twilight crept along the sky as it darkened. A few raindrops splashed onto my windshield, large and heavy as tears. I watched the rain begin slowly, then engulf the parking lot, slanting, bouncing, mixing with the steam that arose from the asphalt. People ran from the stores to their cars using plastic shopping bags as umbrellas.

The rain steadied, and rivulets began running along the cracks in the blacktop. I realized that I did indeed know what I was going to do next. But this rain put a kink in my plans.

Nick and Bertie would be in the movie for at least another half hour. I drove around the parking lot again, this time getting as near to the K-Mart entrance as I could. I ran into the store. The fluorescent lights made everything look surreal, as though all the shelves and displays and racks had been cut from a magazine and pasted on an enormous backdrop.

I bought a box of thirty-gallon garbage bags and, from the stationery department, a bag of rubber bands.

Back in the Bug, I circled the parking lot a final time, and found Nick's pickup. I positioned myself where I could see it. When I turned off the motor the wipers stopped, and the windshield became blurred with rain-drops.

I took out a big, green garbage bag, and with the Swiss army knife I carried, cut a round hole three inches in diameter about a foot from the sealed end of the bag.

Then I just waited.

At last, Nick and Bertie came running through the rain toward the pickup. They weren't holding hands, but he pushed her a little ahead of him, his hand on her waist, as he had so often done with me. They were laughing. She ran her fingers through her hair and shook rain from them before she got in the passenger's side.

I followed the pickup out onto the road. The rain pelted down. Oh, how I wished Nick were driving in the cab alone, with Bertie soaking wet in the truck bed, tossed around like a cord of wood. Everyone had their headlights turned on; cars were shadowy blobs, with bright, white eyes. All I could hear was the watery roar of tires, the whir of the Bug's defroster fan. I was pretty sure where they were going, so I gave them plenty of space.

When the pickup turned into their subdivision, I pulled off the road and waited. They were going to Nick's garage. I'd give them a few minutes to get cozy. I looked at my watch. *Five minutes.*

I swung onto Nick's road, not even looking in the direction of Bertie's house as I passed it. I shut off my headlights and slowly crept down the driveway. It was almost dark. My breath came in gulps.

There was no sign of Mrs. Cunningham's car. And instead of a glow from the garage, there were lights on in the kitchen. *That's where they were.*

I took the camera from my backpack. I put it in the garbage bag, and poked the lens through the hole. Then I secured the garbage bag onto the lens with a rubber band, and doubled on a second rubber band, to make sure the seal was tight. No rain was going to get on this camera. It was completely covered, except for the lens hood, which protected the glass like the brim of a hat.

Quietly, I opened the car door. Then I pressed the camera to my eye, and with my free hand tugged the garbage bag over my head. It stuck to my damp skin going on. I kept pulling until it stretched its length to just below my knees. I was encased in the perfect rain-coat, with a cyclops camera eye to see through.

It was hard to walk. The air was hot and thick inside the garbage bag. Plastic sucked into my mouth with each breath. Since I could only see what the lens saw, I had to scan it toward the ground to select my path. The world was reduced to a small, vapor-fogged rectangle. Stooped low, picking through the soggy grass, I eased up below the kitchen window. I pointed the camera.

Bertie wasn't there. She must have left the room for a minute. Nick balanced on the back legs of his chair, while his feet were propped on the kitchen table. *Susannah would have a fit if anyone sat on a chair like that.* There was a bowl of popcorn in front of him. *Focus.* He took a handful, and with his other hand threw a piece in the air, catching it in his mouth without losing his balance. *Click.*

Then I realized there was absolutely no sign of Bertie.

No chair was pulled up for her, no extra glass of lemonade had been poured. Nick was really by himself.

What did this mean? Why, if they had a chance to be alone, weren't they together? I started to put down the camera, but I couldn't see without it. So I stared at Nick through the lens, feeling bewildered and weirdly disappointed. I'd come to "catch" them. *What if there was no "them" to catch? What if I'd made it all up?*

The wind plastered the garbage bag against the backs of my legs. Streams of water ran down into my socks. *Maybe I ought to get out of here.* I turned around, disoriented and confused. A car was coming. Headlights were bearing down on me. It took me a few seconds to understand what was going on: Mrs. Cunningham. I made two hops to the side, then sank onto my knees behind a bush.

My heart was beating so hard it seemed even the camera was pulsing against my face. *If Mrs. Cunningham were to find me out here it really would be the end. Look what I've done with all that faith she had in me.* Cold mud enveloped my shins as I pressed lower into the ground to escape the headlights. I heard the car door slam. Then I waited, the camera pointed to the ground where the shrub roots and dark grass and mud all merged. I waited for her to see me and scream.

Nothing happened. All I could hear was my own ragged breath inside the garbage bag, the plastic sucking in and out. At last I raised the lens as though it were a periscope and looked around. Mrs. Cunningham's car was parked by the front door. She'd gone in the other way. She probably hadn't even seen the Bug in the driveway turnout. And she hadn't seen me—or seen a giant, green frog behind the bushes.

My heartbeat was calming down, and I knew I should split while I could. But now that I was safe, I couldn't resist another look at Nick. On squat frog legs, I repositioned myself below the window and looked up. He was still alone in his same place at the kitchen table.

He tossed up another kernel of popcorn, and it landed on his chin, then bounced on the floor. *Click.* He looked like an aquarium porpoise with his eager, open mouth, waiting for a keeper to throw him a fish. He missed more and more, and when five in a row had hit him in the nose or pinged off his cheek, he began to laugh.

And then suddenly, it was as though I had turned the camera on myself. Some part of me was sitting on a tree branch, shooting pictures of this scene. I zoomed in on Neela—a huge, muddy-legged, wet frog, crouched outside the window. What could be more ludicrous than a garbage-bag covered, headless person spying on someone throwing popcorn in his mouth and laughing?

I began to laugh with him. He couldn't see or hear me, but I walked back to the Bug, exploding with hilarity, bent over. The ground jiggled through my single, laughter-shaken eye, like a movie camera bumping over a rough road. *What an idiot you've been. What a total lunatic.* I was so glad it was over. I knew now I could let him alone. Let him go out with whomever he wanted. I'd gone as stupidly low as I could go.

Once again, the gates of Arlington Place welcomed me home. I had a James Taylor tape in the cassette player, and I was so relieved that I was helping him out with the chorus of "Shower the People You Love with Love," in my tuneless way. It was over. I hadn't been caught;

no one knew anything about my behavior of the past week. I could return to my life, to Penelope, with just an apology for my abruptness earlier today. *Today? Had this only been one day?*

I would have to tell Susannah something—if she remembered my phone call this afternoon. Anyway, it was time she knew that Nick and I had broken up. She had too many delusions about me: that I was the most popular girl in my school; that I could get into any college if I tried hard enough; that I wanted the same things out of life she did.

Perhaps I could let Aunt Amelia see my Nick photographs.

I slowed and took the first speed bump.

The sides of the street were flooded from the rain, big puddles reaching out from the curb. When Penelope and I were kids, we rushed outside with every summer rain to play in these puddles as though they were swimming holes. When we'd had enough, we'd take long sticks and sweep back the leaves and twigs that clogged the drain grates. We loved the sucking noise the torrents made as water swirled underground. Even now, though the Steiners and other families had backyard swimming pools, the neighborhood kids all came out and played in the summer floods.

I jiggled over the next speed bump and looked up at Penelope's window. The lights were on. Maybe I'd walk down there tonight, if it wasn't too late, and try to get things straight with her. Ahead, all the way to our house, I could see the street lamps, their pink glow fogged by the rain.

As I neared the house, I saw both Susannah's and

Leonard's cars. They were home from dinner. And as I drew closer, I noticed something lying in the street. Something large—or was it a shadow? No, maybe a sack of something, because it looked limp and loose, yet substantial. A sack of what? And with a terrible feeling that made my hands numb, I stopped the car. Opened the door. Got out.

I knew what it was. A person.

The body was near the front of Leonard's car, legs in the pool of flooded water near the curb. It was a man, face down, one arm flung straight out, the other underneath him. His face was twisted away from me. But my headlights shone on him and picked up a gleam from his back pocket. A pint bottle.

Mr. Potter.

I knew I shouldn't touch him, but I didn't know if he was hurt or had just passed out. I called his name. Then I bent over and gently shook his shoulder. I felt caught between terror that he would get up and terror that he wouldn't. He didn't move. I couldn't tell if he was breathing. And then I saw a small stream of blood running from the corner of his mouth, like a slender red snake, slithering away.

I ran to the house, finding my door key as I took the steps two at a time.

"Leonard! Susannah!" I shouted as I opened the door.

"Not so loud, dear," Susannah said from the couch. "You'll wake Leonard."

"It's Mr. Potter," I panted.

"My goodness, sweetie, there's mud all over your legs."

"He's lying in the street. Something awful's happened."

176

Susannah's features lost their after-dinner slackness. Her lips tensed into a thin line, and her eyes became sharper. "Get your father," she ordered.

"Call an ambulance," I cried, as I started up the stairs.

But Leonard was almost downstairs, tying the sash of his seersucker bathrobe as he came.

"It's Mr. Potter, he's lying in the street," I said, looking up at him. His hair was rumpled, his glasses had slid halfway down his nose. His face was puffed and red.

"I knew something was going on, damn it, I knew it!"

"I can't find the number for an ambulance," Susannah called from the living room.

"Call the police," Leonard thundered. "This is absolutely a police matter."

I went to the front door. Someone had to stay with Mr. Potter until help arrived.

"And you know whose fault this is, young lady," Leonard shouted.

"What do you mean?" I asked, stopping short.

"Reginald Potter's been struck down by a hit-and-run driver, that's what I mean."

"He has?" I asked. A terrible fear had come over me as I looked at Leonard's face. Rage made his eyes bulge.

"You bet he has, and you know who's responsible."

"I do?" I said dumbly, the fear growing.

"Ten minutes ago the dogs were barking." He pointed his finger at me thumb up, like a pistol. "So I looked out the bedroom window, and there was some sort of van or pickup truck roaring down the street like a maniac."

I still didn't put it together.

"He did it the other night and he's done it again. Your *boyfriend*," Leonard hissed, drawing his face close to mine. "Your irresponsible, reckless boyfriend, Nick."

177

TEN

Red lights, blue lights swirled on top of the police car and reflected back from the rain-washed street. Neighbors peered from their windows. When the ambulance arrived, they rushed outside in raincoats and spiny umbrellas to form a horseshoe around the accident.

Leonard was inside getting dressed. He wouldn't appear on Arlington Place in his bathrobe. Susannah said she needed a drink to calm down.

"How did it happen?" Mrs. Steiner asked.

I told her I drove home and found Mr. Potter in the street. I didn't dare say Leonard called it a hit-and-run driver. I was too stunned by his accusation.

"I didn't hear anything, did you?" Mrs. Steiner asked her husband.

"I was watching television," he said, shrugging.

"You still might have heard something, Fred. It happened right next to our house."

Mr. Steiner shrugged again.

If Mr. Potter had been hit by a car, it wasn't Nick's. I knew exactly where he'd been every minute since four this afternoon.

"Old Potter's drunk as a skunk day and night, and has been for years," Mrs. Donovan whispered. Petunia strained at her leash, sniffing legs and delicately lapping water from the curb puddles.

"You don't think he could have been mugged, do you?" Mrs. Forbes asked anxiously.

"It's certainly possible. He's a sitting duck, if you ask me."

"Maybe he just fell. Happens all the time to alcoholics," another neighbor said.

Two paramedics loaded the stretcher with Mr. Potter into the ambulance. His arms were crossed over his chest.

"Is he alive?" Mrs. Donovan asked the men.

Mr. Potter, the harmless old man who scared me to death. He'd seemed so threatening, lurching and muttering and singing down the street. Now he was a pathetic, broken-down body.

"He's breathing," a medic answered, latching the rear doors. The ambulance took off down Arlington Place, slowing for each speed bump, the brake lights glowing like hot coals in a wind.

"Should we notify some family member?" Mrs. Steiner asked.

"I can't imagine who," a neighbor said. "He's been living alone ever since his wife died, twenty years ago. Doesn't even have a housekeeper that I know of."

"He doesn't have anyone?" I asked, double-checking. It seemed pitiful that he could be hurt, maybe even die, alone.

"He had a daughter, but she moved away before his wife died," Mrs. Steiner said. "I don't think there's been any sign of her."

"All right," the cop interrupted. "Who knows anything about this?"

I glanced at our house.

"Reginald Potter's been the neighborhood drunk for as long as I can remember," a neighbor told him.

"What happened? Did you see anything?" the cop asked.

I left the circle and started toward the house. Somehow it was comforting to hear fragments about Mr. Potter's life, even if the tiny pieces of information people had made him even more pathetic. Certainly I felt less frightened outside with the neighbors than inside with my parents. But I had to talk to Leonard, before he made a statement to the police.

In the front hall, Leonard was pulling on the rubber field boots he sometimes wore hunting.

"Is poor Mr. Potter going to be all right?" Susannah called from the living room. "Careful Neela, don't drip on the Persian rug."

"I've got to talk to you," I said.

"And I've got to talk to the police," Leonard said, as he stuffed one arm into his yellow slicker.

At that moment, something occurred to me which hadn't before. *I could say nothing and walk upstairs.* I could let Nick get through this one on his own, without a word from me. Oh, the revenge for leaving me; the embarrassment he'd feel having to account for the way he drove out of here the other night; the disgrace of having to go to the police station; the nightmare of having to explain this all to his mother.

I knew I couldn't get him off the hook without exposing myself. Everyone would know about the photographs. If I told the truth about Nick, I was going to be humiliated. The reprieve I'd been granted an hour ago had been cancelled. It had been just a happy little dream: me, the jolly green frog, laughing like a fool outside Nick's window, singing with relief on the way home. Reality was something else. Already the agony of it was whirring in my teeth, like a dentist drilling without an anesthetic.

I was tired of suffering. *Why should I help him? What had he done for me lately?*

At the same time a squeaky, sane little voice in my head told me something else: He'd given me nine months of safety and comfort. During the time we were together, Nick had loved me and I knew it. Breaking up wasn't all his fault. Jealousy did have a lot to do with it—maybe more than I was ready to admit right now. I wanted to blame him—and Bertie—but no longer could I even pretend to know the truth about them.

"Nick couldn't have hit Mr. Potter, Leonard." The right words just rolled out. "I'm absolutely positive. He wasn't anywhere near here tonight."

Susannah leaned against the door frame between the living room and hall. She held a tall glass, and though I didn't know what was in it, I doubted it was ginger ale.

Leonard jammed his other arm into his slicker.

"And just how do you know Nick wasn't here?" Susannah asked. "I thought you called to tell me you'd broken up."

"That's right, we broke up."

"So you weren't with him tonight." Susannah might be dull at crossword puzzles after dinner, but she could hold her memory together when she needed to.

"No."

The horror of this was coming down on me.

Leonard pulled the slicker hood over his head.

"Amelia!" Susannah said. It was an announcement, and Leonard and I both turned toward the stairs. Aunt Amelia was gripping the banister, descending slowly. She wore rubber thong sandals, as though she were going to the beach, and over her pink-striped nightgown, a clear plastic raincoat. On her head was a see-through rain hat with scalloped edges that drooped down on her forehead.

"What's going on out there? Ambulance, police . . ."

"Nothing, Amelia," Susannah said, trying to sound soothing, as though she were talking to a small child. "It's all over."

"It certainly isn't over," Leonard said. "I'm on my way out to tell the police what I know."

"Which is?" Aunt Amelia asked.

"That Reginald Potter's been injured—maybe killed—by a hit-and-run driver."

"How dreadful," Aunt Amelia gasped.

"And I have every reason to suspect—"

"Leonard," I interrupted. "You don't have any reason. Nick wasn't near here tonight. Don't you believe me?"

Aunt Amelia looked back and forth at both of us.

"We're trying to get this straight," Susannah said, as she set her glass down on the hall table. She snatched it up again and rubbed at the wet ring with her forearm. "Leonard says the dogs were making a ruckus, which they never do unless there's some disturbance."

Right, I thought. *Like the Steiner boys playing outside, or any innocent person walking by on the sidewalk.*

"And he saw a truck that looked like Nick's truck, roaring down the street like a maniac."

The both used the same phrase over and over. Was that what happened when you'd been married so long?

"Neela—" Susannah nodded at me—"says she knows it wasn't Nick. But she wasn't with him tonight, so I don't understand how she can be so sure." She looked around, with a barely suppressed smile for her own summation.

"It wasn't Nick," I said firmly. "I don't know if the truck Leonard saw really hit Mr. Potter, or if he just fell—or what."

"Wait a minute," Leonard said. "Why do you think he would 'just fall'?"

"Because he's drunk every night," I said. "Loaded. Polluted. Every single night."

"Oh, I don't know about that," Susannah said, turning aside. "He gets a little carried away now and then, but not every night."

"Susannah, he's the neighborhood drunk and everyone knows it. You've even said that. All the neighbors were talking about it outside."

"And that's where I'm going," Leonard said, reaching for the door knob.

I swiveled between Leonard and the door, leaning against it, the knob pressing into my back. "Don't. I'll tell you how I know it wasn't Nick."

Blood pounded in my temples. I felt my mouth go dry. *This was going to be harder than it had been to tell them I was failing eighth grade science; harder than making my campaign speech for student council; harder than giving a toast at my cousin Elizabeth's enormous wedding.*

"Nick went to the movies this afternoon." Tears formed behind my eyes. I swallowed and went on. "Then

183

he went home. Then he sat in his kitchen alone and ate popcorn. That's where he was when I came home and found Mr. Potter."

"But you said you weren't with him," Susannah said for the umpteenth time.

"I wasn't." A tear leaked out, and I angrily wiped it away. "I followed him."

"What do you mean?"

"I trailed him. Spied on him."

"Oh, that's preposterous," she said. "We—you—don't do things like that."

Leonard was looking at me with a new kind of anger. It was calmer, stonier, heavier. "You followed him," he repeated. "That is indeed very hard to believe." I knew I was headed down the road to the ultimate punishment: his grave disappointment in me.

I glanced over at Aunt Amelia. She had taken off her rain hat and, from her vantage on the stairs, was looking at me calmly, without the disapproval I expected. It seemed clear, in those few seconds, that I could trust her. If she'd seen any of my photographs, or knew anything about what had been going on, she wasn't about to betray me.

"Is this something you do often, *spy* on people?" Susannah asked in a tone of disbelief.

"Just Nick," I said, aware my head was down and I was probably mumbling.

"And have you done this before?" she continued in the same tone.

Before I could answer, Leonard cut in. "I'm not sure a word of this is true," he said. "I have a feeling you're making this up to protect your boyfriend."

184

I flinched at the irony of the word *boyfriend*.

He pulled himself up again and moved toward me and the door. I didn't change position and, blocking the exit, looked him in the eye. "I have proof."

Now Aunt Amelia was shaking her head. "None of this is my business," she announced, and started back up the stairs.

"Stay, Amelia," Leonard ordered, in the same voice he commanded the dogs.

"I have no intention of it. I'm not going to watch the two of you trounce this child."

"Aunt Amelia!" I cried, sensing my only possible support was pulling out.

"You know where to find me," she said. She continued up the stairs, but looked over her shoulder, until her eyes locked with mine. "And don't forget: You can maintain your own dignity."

I'd been on the edge of running to the backpack and showing them the camera. I'd felt the only way out was to hurl my prints at them. But there was something about the way Aunt Amelia said "dignity" that made me hold off.

"So where's this 'proof'?" Leonard asked. He'd taken off his hood.

My fingernails were digging into my palms; I unclenched my hands. I knew that deep breaths could help center you, and I needed them now. I tried to make myself grow taller, as Aunt Amelia sometimes did. "It's in my camera. I'll have proof in two hours."

"That's not good enough. What do you need two hours for?" Leonard said.

"Did you take my Polaroid?" Susannah muttered.

"How many times have I told you not to borrow things without asking me?" She opened the drawer of the oak table, where she always kept the camera. She closed it quickly.

Dignity. "I need two hours because I have to develop film and make a few prints."

They both stared at me.

At last Leonard took off his slicker. "If I don't like the 'proof,' I'm calling the police. Just because I've decided not to go out there this minute doesn't mean I've changed my mind about that kid."

Trays were filled with developer, stop bath, fixer. Everything was ready for the final step except for the film, which had been developed but still hung drying. I'd rushed into the darkroom with a mere nod to Aunt Amelia. Now—I feared—she was waiting for me. Waiting for an explanation.

"In here," she called from the bedroom.

"Hi," I said, feeling more shy than I ever had in my life.

She was in a corner, bent over the stack of large, flat boxes. "Oh good. You're just the one I need to give me a hand." She straightened up. "Bring this box of prints out into the sitting room, will you please? I'll need them all eventually, but let's just take them one at a time."

Not a word about me. No questions about spying on anyone.

"Good," Aunt Amelia said when I'd put the heavy box on the table. "A little dusty, huh? Here's a towel to wipe our hands before we touch the photographs."

She opened the top of the gray, linen-covered box. There was tissue paper over the top print. "Acid-free

186

paper," she said. "Finished prints are valuable and must be protected from dust and scratches." She slid the paper aside, and we both gazed at the black-and-white photograph.

A woman sat at a loom, weaving, in a dark, mud-walled room. She was old, and every wrinkle, every pore in her face was distinct, shining as though her skin had been burnished with silver. Her hair glowed white, while the background faded into rich, velvet black.

"I had to work for that one," Aunt Amelia said quietly. "It took weeks of talking to her in my terrible Spanish before she trusted me enough to let me make photographs. And then the only light in the room came from the door. But it's a strong image, isn't it?"

I didn't want to speak, I just wanted to sink into the calm of the photograph. The old weaver looked as though she'd sat at the loom since the world began, and would stay there, serene and beautiful, forever.

"I'd be so happy if I could ever take a picture like that," I said at last.

"Well, you will, my dear. If you want to, you can take better ones."

We both sat quietly for a few more seconds, looking at the photograph.

"Now," she said briskly, "here's my chore for the next few weeks. And I could use your help." She placed the print on the table, and took the tissue off the next one. "A small museum in Texas has been pestering me for a show of this old Mexican work, and I've decided to do it. I know you're busy with your own projects, but I thought your eye would be valuable in helping me pick prints to send them."

"But I don't know enough . . ."

187

"Nonsense. You've spent a great deal of time in the darkroom. I saw your first prints, and they showed sensitivity and promise."

"You haven't seen anything of mine lately," I said.

"You haven't wanted to show me anything. And that's perfectly acceptable. It's your work." She'd taken the paper off a lush mountain landscape, and gone on to the next picture.

I checked my watch. "I've got a few prints to do right now. But I want you to see them when I'm done."

"Fine," she said. "I'll be here."

In the darkroom, I printed a contact sheet. There, the size of postage stamps, were the pictures: Uncle Sam's, a confusion of textures and patterns; the Cineplexten, doors, windows, coming attractions, all rectangles inside rectangles; a dozen shots of Nick, head tilted back, tossing popcorn in his mouth. No pictures of the giant, green frog waiting below Nick's window.

I made the prints. The blacks weren't as deep as Aunt Amelia's, nor were the white highlights as clean, but they were good, crisp prints. And I found they no longer had the electric, fiery meaning they'd had when I took them. They were pictures and I cared about them and that was enough.

I brought out the box of prints I'd stashed on a shelf under the enlarger and went out to Aunt Amelia. I sat on the floor and began to spread them out.

"Oh no, dear, not the floor," Aunt Amelia cried. "Here, up on the table. Your work must be treated with respect." She moved her own to one side.

"Come on, Aunt Amelia, these aren't anything special."

188

"They are indeed, every one of them. Now let's have a look."

Aunt Amelia studied my prints. She started at the beginning. She wasn't critical—she didn't ask why there was a white spot on the corner of this one, or why that one seemed a little blurred—but she took her time examining each one. She talked about them as though they were important. She said they had passion.

"And this one," she said, holding up a print of Nick playing the guitar, "I suspect he is your young man."

"Was. Used to be."

I found myself telling her about Nick. I didn't plan anything I said, didn't think how embarrassing this was, just let it come. I described my envy for his talents and his energy and his ability to get a job and his understanding mother. I told her how betrayed I felt when he bought a truck, although I knew I'd already lost him. I told her about Bertie and spying on them. I even admitted I'd gotten drunk to try to make the hurt go away.

I felt as though I'd burst a giant, painful blister, and let all the yuck drain out.

Aunt Amelia sat quietly and didn't ask questions, even when I got tied up in my own words. I could hardly get it out, but I talked about the sex, and how I'd tried to hold Nick that way. I told her how Penelope had seen everything coming, and said I was *clinging*.

"I've been clinging, too," she said, nodding.

I looked at her straight on, without asking the question. I wanted to give her the same understanding and respect she'd shown me.

"Oliver. Memory," she said, smiling faintly. "I've been clinging to memory."

Finally I told her about today. I cried a little, thinking of the shame of it.

"And you promised Leonard you'd have 'proof' in two hours?" she asked.

I looked at my watch. I checked Aunt Amelia's wall clock to be sure my own watch hadn't gone crazy. It was one-thirty in the morning. Three and a half hours had passed.

"I'll see you in the morning," she said, as I jumped up.

"Eight-thirty?" I asked.

"In the darkroom. And be prepared to get technical."

I ran downstairs, the five best prints from tonight in my hand. My proof. The Tiffany lights were on in the living room: I was expected.

But Susannah wasn't in her usual post on the uncomfortable Victorian couch. Leonard wasn't in the living room either. Two glasses, empty except for the remnants of an ice cube, were sweating into coasters on the coffee table. The table had a red *sold* tag attached to its leg, and so had the desk and a side chair, thanks to Susannah's tea.

I opened the door and looked outside. Both their cars were parked in exactly the same place they had been earlier. I was wrong: I wasn't expected. They'd forgotten about the 'proof' and gone to bed.

It had stopped raining and the curb puddles had drained, the way they always did. For the time being, there was no Mr. Potter to stagger and shout his way down the street, but he might be back. I didn't want him to die. There were better ways to deal with him than to hide, and I'd have to learn them.

From the kennel in back, one of the dogs started to

bay but cut it off in mid-howl as though he'd awakened himself from a doggie nightmare.

I looked down the block, following the street lamps, to Penelope's house. No lights were on there, but I knew I'd find her home tomorrow. Beyond her house, at the end of the block, were the gates of Arlington Place. When I was a kid, I imagined shutting both gates at either end, cutting Arlington Place off from the world, the way a moat sealed off a castle. The gates were supposed to protect us. They couldn't do that, I knew. Everything was changing, and always would. But I could take care of myself.

I studied the prints in my hand. There was my proof.